A Most Unlikely Man:
A Tale of Resistance

by

J.P. Rieger

BLUE
CEDAR
PRESS

Wichita, Kansas

DEDICATION: To my Kristin - my Everything!

He needed to see his grandson, Nathan, immediately. It was finally time to tell the story. No, not a story, his biography. *No. Too noble sounding.* His life. A time in his life. His history. *That's it.* And his history wasn't a "story." It was his reality, an indelible part of his being, his core. A part he had brushed aside and cloistered away, but yet central to his person. This would be his last Passover. It was time.

He was never able to tell his own son, who he had outlived. *Why?* Probably because dredging up those times brought such immense sadness, such fear. As though speaking about those times would bring them back to life, would somehow bring the past to the present, a past he had so gratefully left behind.

He had emigrated to America with his young bride. He had been determined to start anew, to raise an American family. Yes, a family committed to the Jewish faith and traditions. But a family otherwise willing to assimilate, to live the American Dream.

Through the shaded, yellowing vision of nearly one-hundred-year-old eyes, he saw Nathan and his young family enter his room. He watched the nursing assistant, Clarissa, follow close behind them.

Nathan's grandfather lay comfortably in his recliner, covered with a light blanket. The television was on, but the sound was muted. "Hi, Saba! How have you been, today? Look, Rachel is here too with Brian and Judith!" Nathan gently squeezed his grandfather's shoulder.

Rachel spoke loudly, because Saba was nearly deaf. "You're looking fine, Saba! Kids, come here and say hi to Saba." Rachel grasped Saba's cold, liver-spotted hand. The chilliness surprised her, but she didn't flinch and continued to hold his hand.

The children moved closer, cautiously. They said, "Hi, Saba," in near unison. They saw him slowly raise his other, shaking hand from the blanket to wave back a greeting.

"Hello, children. Hello, Rachel and my Nathan."

Nathan turned to the nursing assistant. He had forgotten her name again, even though he had vowed to himself last time to remember. She was, by far, the best assistant they had hired. And then he remembered. "Clarissa, how has my grandpa been today? Did they deliver his seder meal?"

"Yes, Mr. Levin. About a half hour ago."

"Thanks, and please just call me Nate. Was he able to take off the sealed wrapper?"

"Yes. He did well and finished most of it." She nodded in affirmation. "He's been asking about you all day. He's been saying, 'Nathan, Nathan' a whole lot. He's also been asking about Mrs. Fogle."

"Mrs. Fogle? You mean another resident here?"

"No. I asked around, and there aren't any Fogles here. He's been saying, 'Wife 'a Fogle, wife 'a Fogle,' all day, so I thought he meant a Mrs. Fogle … you know, Mr. Fogle's wife? Like he maybe knew a Mr. Fogle and was asking about Mr. Fogle's wife. But there aren't any Fogles here."

"Uh. Okay. Gosh, I don't think we know any Fogles either." He looked toward Rachel, who shrugged. "Anyway, thanks for always taking such good care of my grandpa, Clarissa. We appreciate you!"

"All good, Mr. Nate!"

Nathan saw that the kids were getting restless. He wanted them to know and love their great-grandfather, but not to be uncomfortable near him. Not to be afraid just because he was so very old. Or because he had a German accent and sometimes spoke in German. "Rach, how about you guys say bye-bye to Saba and meet me in the lounge area in just a couple minutes?"

"Okay, Naty. Kids, come see Saba and say goodbye."

The children walked slowly toward the recliner, afraid to get too close. "Bye-bye, Saba!"

Rachel chimed in, "Sweet Pesach, Saba. We love you!" She kissed him gently on his cold forehead.

With the room cleared, Nathan brought out his worn copy of the Haggadah and sat on the bedside. He would narrate just portions of the Maggid, because Saba already had the seder meal. He needed to get his family home in time for their own Passover preparations. He held Saba's hand and read aloud about the Egyptians' inhumane treatment of the people of Israel and the Israelites who cried out to the God of their fathers for deliverance. And how the Lord God delivered his people from Egypt.

But Saba shook his head and rasped. "No. Nathan. I must tell you something. Something I did not tell even your father. About me. My story. And about a man. You must listen and tell your children this story. It will then be their story." He reached for his copy of the Haggadah, which was leather-bound and worn. He pulled from it a sheaf of yellowing papers.

"I wrote this years ago but could never share it with anyone. I couldn't bear to. But before I leave this earth, I must pass it on to my family. Will you read it with me, please?"

Nathan unfolded the papers and smoothed them, curious. He could see from the irregular letters, certain ones higher than others, that they were made from an old typewriter. Something his grandfather had shared with no one? This must be important.

"Of course, Saba. I will read this with you," he said, settling himself in the metal chair beside Grandfather's recliner.

...

In 1940, the Alsace region of France was forcibly annexed into the German Reich. The Nazis established the Natzweiler-Struthof concentration camp in the nearby mountains for forced labor, medical experimentation, and exterminations. Following the August, 1944 liberation of Paris, the Nazis, fearing Allied advances, transported all remaining prisoners of Natzweiler-Struthof to its satellite camps. By mid-September, only a minimal Nazi presence remained. In late November, Allied forces reached the camp and found it completely deserted.

Early October, 1944

Isadore Levinsky leaned his flattened palms against the grimy wall of the boxcar. He felt the train slowly pulling to a stop. In his prior life as a young and determined school principal, he would have cursed the slowness, the awful eternity that seemed to pass before a train would come to its final halt. Now it no longer mattered. Every moment he lived as a prisoner replicated that same eternity. He took comfort knowing that he would die. *Soon enough, but perhaps not today.* He heard the pained, low groans of his fellow prisoners mixed in with the rumbling sounds of the brakes. Most of the prisoners were huddled on the crowded floor among the pools of urine and feces, too weak to stand. Some were already dead. He looked down at the sets of sunken eyes of the two men who had succumbed to starvation and lack of water. *They're free now.*

He was alive by chance. He happened to be by the door that first day of the journey and grabbed one of the two rock hard, stale loaves of bread thrown through the door by the German soldier. Loaves intended to feed the entire boxcar of about thirty men. He gnawed through nearly an entire loaf before the other prisoners threatened to kill him. The bread gave him a head start, though. He knew to always be near the door when the train began to slow. The others learned, too, but were too weak to position themselves ahead of him. He didn't like that he consumed far more than his share. These were Jews, just like him. His brothers. But he desired to live. He couldn't help that.

The last jerking motion of the brakes nearly knocked him to the ground. He looked down at the two corpses at his feet. They had been dragged there by fellow prisoners through excruciating acts of will. He hadn't touched the dead men. He knew he would have to, soon enough.

The German soldier slid back the door, revealing the dusk and its nearly extinguished daylight. Two other soldiers held their rifles forward, ready to fire upon the men.

"Any dead?"

Levinsky responded. "These two." He pointed down at his feet.

The German corporal peered into the car and saw that, except for Levinsky, none of the prisoners would be strong enough to assist. He turned to a short soldier a few paces behind. "Hammel, pull those two dead Jews off with the help of that Jew." He pointed to Levinsky.

The short man looked up, angrily. "Why me? Why do I have to touch a dead Jew?"

Levinsky heard the group of soldiers laugh loudly.

"Why you? Because I'm a corporal and I said so, baby boy. Someday when you become an officer, then you can make someone else do your shit work!" More laughter.

Hammel pulled a short club from his uniform coat and pushed it into Levinsky's chest. "Jew, help me pick up these two."

He put the club back in his coat. He watched as Levinsky picked up the first corpse by the shoulders, swinging its legs forward toward Hammel. The corpse's bony legs fluttered within his tattered, striped prison uniform.

Levinsky looked into the face of the corpse. Maybe he knew him from Hamburg? Probably not. He didn't really know any of the men in the boxcar. They had been assembled piecemeal along the way. He knew only that they were Jews like him.

Levinsky took a closer look at the short soldier and his clownish, overly large uniform. He was a child. Probably thirteen, maybe fourteen. He could tell because he had taught and counseled many such young men before he was taken. Jews, of course, not other Germans. *And that's the irony. I am a German. I was born here. I obeyed German law. I loved my homeland just like these Nazis pretend to. But now I am just a Jew. A Jew taken away to starve and die.*

"Young soldier, grab his feet and pull him off. I will push him toward you."

Hammel grabbed the dead man's feet and pulled him off of the boxcar. No struggle because the corpse was feather-light. The two repeated the same procedure for the second corpse. The boy then grabbed each corpse by its collar, one in each hand, and dragged the corpses, slowly, to a mound of dead bodies several yards away from the tracks and water cistern. He yelled at the black vultures that clawed and pecked at what was left of the bodies on the mound. The birds looked at him with curiosity, but didn't move away. Hammel didn't bother to drag the corpses onto the top of the mound of mostly unclothed shells. Along the bottom was good enough. He knew that the mounds were typically incinerated. But he also knew that gasoline within the Reich was in short supply.

The corporal saw that the boy had completed his task. "Over here, Hammel. We will let them have water from the trough."

The corporal pointed at Levinsky. "You, Jew, help these other Jews and yourself to get water." He pointed to an ancient wood trough located next to a stone cistern. "Stay away from the cistern or you will die. That's for us. Only the trough for you."

Levinsky hopped down and held his hand out into the boxcar. "If any of you need water and can make it over here, come."

Slowly, painfully, the prisoners capable of standing tried to do so. Some immediately fell back down to the ground out of weakness. A few began to crawl their way past the immobile prisoners to the door. Levinsky helped the first man out of the boxcar and walked with him, holding him by the torso to prevent his falling over. As he passed the cistern, Levinsky saw movement in his periphery and glanced over at the mound of corpses. An alabaster white creature moving on top of the pile. Maybe a gull? Beautiful white. It had scared away the vultures. He thought for an instant it could be a man, naked. Pale white. He decided it couldn't possibly be and quickly looked away. He pushed himself and the prisoner toward the trough. A German soldier stood guard nearby, waiting. Levinsky dared not look back to the mound again with the guard so close by. In the distance, he heard the German corporal ordering Hammel to assist other prisoners who had successfully crawled to the door.

Levinsky cupped his hands and took his own drink of water from the foul trough. *Water should be tasteless. This is not.* But he knew he had to drink, notwithstanding whatever bad things were in the water. And he had tasted far worse water. *Far worse.* He heard the young soldier, Hammel, yelling and pulling a prisoner off the train to the laughter of the other soldiers. Levinsky saw the armed guard look toward the laughter and decided to steal one last glance at the mound. Nothing. As he turned back toward the trough, he felt the hands of the other prisoner grab at his throat. Levinsky instinctively yelled, "Help!" although the man's grasp was impossibly weak.

Immediately, the guard took the butt of his rifle and smacked it into the face of the prisoner, knocking him from Levinsky. The commotion attracted the attention of the other German soldiers who raced away from the boxcar and toward the trough.

The corporal shouted, "What's going on?"

The soldier standing guard reported. "This stupid Jew tried to choke the Jew that helped him." He pointed to the prisoner he had struck with his rifle. The prisoner had curled into the fetal position to avoid further blows. His gasping groans could barely be heard.

"Leave it to the Jews to try to kill each other. They don't need us, do they?" The corporal smiled as the group of soldiers laughed obligatorily.

"All right. No more water for these idiots. Hammel, get these two and your own back onto the car. We have a schedule to keep."

Levinsky helped his prisoner up and began walking him slowly back to the train. He knew why he was attacked. He didn't care. He would continue to do whatever necessary to survive. Although he wasn't sure why.

Hammel walked next to them with his own prisoner. He scowled at Levinsky. "Hurry up, Jew. You're wasting time." As they approached the boxcar, Hammel looked up to see a prisoner standing inside, holding a bucket filled with feces.

"Sir, would you allow me to empty this bucket and then bring water back from the trough? These men are dying of thirst, sir. Please?"

Hammel was about to yell "no" when he heard the corporal laugh behind him. "Sure, Jew, if you Jew dogs want to eat and drink your own filth, who am I to stop you? Hammel, help this stupid Jew to the trough."

Levinsky looked closely at the prisoner. He hadn't thought any of them would have the strength to stand up, let alone stand with a full bucket. He made a mental note to watch that one. Especially if that prisoner tried to get to the doors before him at the next stop.

…

The night passed slowly as the train achingly ascended a series of steep, rolling hills. All throughout the night, the sounds of aircraft filled the skies, punctuated by nearby explosions. Levinsky knew these were the sounds of American bombers, not the sounds of airstrikes by German aircraft over France.

The next stop turned out to be their final stop, a small railway station. A soldier slid open the door. The corporal yelled, "Everybody out. Hurry up!" He pointed to Levinsky and the man who had brought back the bucket of water. "You two, help the other Jews out. Make sure everyone can walk. Otherwise, they'll be shot."

Levinsky disembarked. He was glad that the stop was an actual railway station and not an empty field or lime-covered pit. The Nazis were not likely to execute them here at least. He saw the railway sign: "Rothau." He didn't know the place but figured, with the dense forest and nearby mountains, they were in Alsace, possibly near Strasbourg.

He watched most of the German soldiers reenter the passenger section of the train for further deployment. Only a few remained behind with the prisoners. He saw a truck in the waiting. He knew he would not be riding in the truck.

Another man in the boxcar had perished overnight. Levinsky looked at his face. *The man that tried to strangle me.* The corporal ordered Hammel to remove the corpse and take it behind the station to an incineration pile.

...

After great effort, Levinsky and the other man managed to get the other prisoners out of the car. The corporal pulled Levinsky over and stood him at the main road to the station. "See that road, Jew? That's where you Jews must walk. A nice uphill path. Only two or three miles. Hope you enjoy the climb!" The corporal laughed. "Assemble the other Jews and start walking. We'll be right behind you in the truck."

Levinsky looked behind to see the tattered assembly of nearly walking corpses. Several were only able to crawl.

The corporal yelled loudly, "Everyone must walk or die." Immediately, the men who were crawling tried to right themselves. The man who had brought water in the bucket helped a particularly weak man to his feet, carrying him along by his waist.

The steep road challenged the men, but they pushed on, motivated by the sound of the German truck right behind them, ready to run them down. Levinsky didn't mind the walk. He was just glad to be free of the train and its constant noises and foul odors. The forest was quite beautiful and the air pure.

After ascending an impossibly steep hill, Levinsky heard a cry behind him and looked around. One of the men had stumbled, too weak to stand. The man who had brought water in the bucket ran over to the man and tried to raise him up. But the effort failed. The prisoner was too weak to even hold onto the man's waist. He fell a second time.

The corporal shouted, "Hammel, drag him off to the side."

Hammel grabbed the dying man by the collar and dragged him to a culvert alongside the road. The corporal and a private walked over. The corporal removed his sidearm from his holster and fired one shot into the base of the skull of the dying man. The man still made slight movements. The corporal re-holstered his gun.

"Aren't you going to shoot him again, sir? He's still moving."

"No, Bauer. We can't spare the ammunition. The wolves will finish him soon enough."

The ragtag group finally made it to the crest of the hill. The destination, another concentration camp. Levinsky had seen larger camps. He had been in Stutthof the year before until transferred to a smaller camp. But a concentration camp was a concentration camp. *Better than a death camp.*

The corporal disembarked and directed the prisoners to line up in a single file in front of the gate. He provided a lazy salute to the gatekeeper and passed over his documentation. The soldier at the gatehouse glanced through the paperwork. He promptly exited the gatehouse and opened the gate. The corporal looked more closely and was startled to see that the gatekeeper was a lieutenant. He saluted, robustly.

"Heil Hitler, Lieutenant. Beg the lieutenant's pardon for not realizing your rank, sir."

"Heil. That's okay, Corporal. The colonel asked that I meet your squad here personally on his behalf. I am Lieutenant Magnus, Assistant to the colonel. Welcome to Natzweiler-Struthof. The colonel is occupied at this moment but sends his greetings. These

Jews are to occupy the B barracks." Magnus pointed to one of the smaller buildings. "I'll meet you there. Please follow."

"Jews, follow the lieutenant." The prisoners trudged forth slowly as the truck followed behind.

Levinsky noticed something odd. Except for themselves, the camp seemed empty. A ghost town. He wasn't sure why.

The men settled into the barracks, a dismal wood-framed prison with no beds and a filthy straw-covered floor. One tiny wood burning stove served to heat the room. But the wood fuel had been exhausted long ago by the former occupants. The stove was ice cold. Four filthy buckets were stowed in the corner for waste. Empty buckets for water were stored in the opposite corner.

Although it was daylight and the wood framing of the barracks allowed a great deal of light to pass through, several of the prisoners quickly fell asleep on the cold ground, exhausted by the morning's journey and lack of food.

...

Private Bauer dreaded the conversation. "Corporal, I must report some failure on my part in my accounting for the men."

"Don't tell me a man is missing, Private?"

"No sir. Somehow, I miscounted previously, and we have one more man than I had thought."

"Ha! An extra Jew? Well, I wouldn't worry, Bauer. I doubt that a Jew would voluntarily imprison himself just to get a ride in the boxcar."

"No sir, of course."

"Ah. You probably forgot the Jew I shot at the station. He's dead by now, I'm sure. Just strike one more off the list."

"Yes sir. But I did account for the dead Jew."

"Okay, Bauer. Just correct the count. The sergeant will be arriving here soon and won't care exactly how many we have. Understand? Say nothing and forget about it."

"Yes sir."

...

The day wore on, and the exhausted prisoners sat in gloomy silence. The man who had gotten water in the bucket watched Levinsky position himself next to the door. The bucket man stood and spoke loudly.

"Everyone. We will have a system for food. Each of us will share equally in whatever food and water is provided."

Levinsky scowled and continued to stand by the door.

"Sir, if you accept the food by the door, you are required to share it equally among all the men. Do you understand this?"

Levinsky barked back, "Who the hell do you think you are? Who put you in charge?"

"My name is Otto. Otto Beck. What is your name, sir?"

"Levinsky. Isadore Levinsky. I don't have any superiors here, so I don't abide by any rules."

"Levinsky. I know that name. There were Levinskys in my school. Fine people. Good family. And I agree. No one here has a superior. We are all equal. Hence, we will share what we receive, equally."

"Go to hell, Beck."

"We are nearly there, Isadore. But not quite. Now, let me stress the importance of sharing the food and water. Every man here is important. Each man must survive this imprisonment. We must work together. Help one another. That is how we survive. That is how we'll win."

The prisoners began to pay attention. Several mumbled inquisitively.

"Win? Idiot. Go shit yourself."

"We can win, Isadore. We will win. The Nazis presume that we will all die here, whether from work, exposure, or starvation. If each of us, and I count twenty-two, survive … if we live … we win. We will have beaten them. And then we will walk out of this camp as free men."

The murmuring sounds—sounds of great surprise—grew.

"Unlikely, Beck. Most unlikely. You're an idiot. But I'll tell you what. I'll agree to take an equal share of the food and water, provided that you take none. How does that suit you?"

"That's acceptable, Lev. May I call you 'Lev'? I'm usually not that hungry or thirsty."

Levinsky spat on the ground and laughed. "Okay, idiot Beck. As you wish!"

…

Sergeant Wittmer and Corporal Emmerich assembled with Lieutenant Magnus in the colonel's spartan outer office.

Magnus pointed over his shoulder to the closed door behind his desk. "Gentlemen, Colonel Rettmund is again occupied, but has placed me under his charge to assist you in this relocation. No doubt, your quarters in the officers' residence building are sufficient?"

Wittmer and Emmerich responded together. "Yes sir."

Wittmer spoke. "Sir, we were hoping you could explain the relocation. Has this camp been abandoned?"

Magnus absent-mindedly removed his tiny wire spectacles, cleaning them with a small satin cloth. "Abandoned? No. But I understand your observations." He swept his hand and glasses into the air. "The camp was cleared out just last month. Berlin ordered that all prisoners be moved to sub-camps for ultimate relocation to Dachau for efficiency purposes. At Dachau, the populations will be consolidated in order to make best use of those facilities. Only the colonel, myself, and some civilian workers remain stationed here. And, oh yes, and Captain Gessert, rotates throughout the many sub-camps and is posted here periodically. And occasionally our camp is inspected by Captain Gessert's commanding officer, Major Lindauer. The major is a rather exacting man. His nephew is Gestapo." Magnus rolled his eyes. "At present, the sub-camps are filled to capacity, hence your relocation here."

"Of course, sir. Are there new orders from Berlin with respect to these prisoners? There are so few of them."

"No, Sergeant. Just the standing orders. The Reich believes these Jew criminals could be put to some future use beyond mere factory and field work because of their alleged skills or learning. While I personally doubt that, we of course, continue to honor the standing order."

"Of course, sir."

"Subject, of course, to the Jews doing routine work around the camp and subject, of course, to the consequences of disciplinary measures and ordinary attrition. Many of these ignorant Jews lack the will to live and simply die. And should a Jew die as a result of disciplinary measures, so be it. We cannot control these factors."

"Yes sir. Understood."

"But, enough of formalities. Both of you must join me this evening in the officers' dining hall. This camp was once a hotel and recreation facility. The dining hall is one of its few remaining comforts. We don't have quite the coterie of staff to wait on us due to the prior relocation, but I promise that the food and wine will be more than satisfactory."

...

Corporal Emmerich and Sergeant Wittmer dined pleasantly with the lieutenant. Afterward, they rounded up Bauer and Hammel to assist in feeding the prisoners. They had nearly forgotten. They would join Bauer and Hammel after a smoke outside the prison barracks.

Bauer unlocked the barracks door. Four hanging electric bulbs illuminated the room, save its corners. Hammel dragged in a small metal barrel filled halfway with a thin gruel. A tin cup, tied to the barrel handle, was submerged into the gruel. Bauer held his rifle against the prisoners to encourage orderly dining. Hammel left to retrieve a second barrel filled with water.

"Form a line here, men." He watched, surprised as each man drank just one cup of gruel and moved again to the back of the line. He noticed that one—the Jew with the bucket—sat against the wall simply smiling.

Hammel managed to drag the water barrel inside the barracks. He and Bauer both watched as, again, the men took turns. No man tried to take a second cup without first getting back to the end of the line. And again, the bucket man remained seated.

Bauer spoke. "You. Get up and take water. That's an order."

Beck stood. "Sir, I will do so only if Mr. Levinsky authorizes such."

"What are you talking about! Get yourself water, fool!"

Beck looked over to Levinsky who nodded his head "yes" quickly and decisively. Beck nodded back in appreciation and got into the back of the line.

Emmerich and Wittmer enjoyed their casual smoke outside the barracks.

"Sergeant, do you think the rumors are true? That this camp was evacuated because the Americans and French are close by? Or maybe a Russian contingent?"

Wittmer exhaled. "Who knows? Very odd. Shuttling these worthless Jews around, wasting our time. But you've heard the bombings like the rest of us." He shrugged.

After the prisoners exhausted the contents of the barrels, Emmerich and Wittmer entered the barracks.

Emmerich laughed. "We knew you Jews were finished by the noise of you trying to scrape the last bit of water out of the metal barrel with the metal cup! Dumb animals."

Wittmer laughed along. "Okay, stupid Jews. I am Sergeant Wittmer. Don't make trouble. Did you notice on the way in? They have a nice gas chamber and small crematorium just waiting to serve you!"

More laughter.

Beck raised his hand. "Sir, I was wondering. Although we are thankful for the food and water, by chance do you have table scraps left over from your meal? Perhaps if you did, one of your staff could just bring the tablecloth and shake it out in here. We would be grateful for those crumbs and scraps."

Wittmer laughed. "Table scraps? Those are for the animals, the dogs. Not you Jews."

"I beg your pardon, sir, but I do not believe that there are any dogs here. I've heard no barking or baying throughout the day. Perhaps they were moved when everything else was moved. Because this camp is quite empty, as you no doubt have noticed."

With that, Wittmer motioned to Bauer to hand him his rifle. He walked calmly over to Beck, striking him, violently, with the butt of the rifle. Beck crumbled down to his knees, holding himself steady with his hands. The impact against Beck's face bloodied his nose.

"Impudent Jew! Our camp is none of your business! That goes for every Jew here!"

Beck rallied and stood again, holding his nose with one hand. "Begging your pardon again, sir. I am actually not a Jew. I'm a full-blood German just like you."

Wittmer looked over to Emmerich, astonished. Before either could speak, Beck continued.

"My name is Otto Beck. But I am not here wrongfully. You see, according to the laws of the Third Reich I am far worse than a Jew. I was convicted of treason, for being an anarchist and a socialist. For refusing military service. But actually I am just a pacifist. That makes me much worse than these men. These men are here unfairly. They committed no crime other than to be born a Jew. They never received a trial or conviction. I, on the other hand, a convicted pacifist, belong here."

Emmerich shouted, "Pacifist? You mean queer! Homosexual! That's what 'pacifist' means in the Reich! Yes, piece of shit. You are worse than a Jew!" He laughed haughtily.

Beck smiled. "Those are just words, Corporal. Not accurate words, but words nevertheless. But words, like these men, are also innocent. They cannot control how they are used. And, thankfully, they do not hurt."

Emmerich waited for Wittmer to strike at Beck again. When he did not, Emmerich pulled his sidearm out of its holster and prepared to shoot. He felt Wittmer's hand touch his arm. "No, Corporal. Let the Jews take care of him. They despise queers too. Even more so a gentile queer!" Wittmer laughed again. "Hammel, Bauer, make sure there's no latrine break for these Jews, thanks to the queer. They use the buckets only."

"Yes sir!"

The prisoners watched the four Nazi soldiers exit the barracks. They heard the metallic sound of the door latch being engaged and locked. They sat quietly, still astonished by what they had heard Beck say, by the fact that he said it at all.

Levinsky spoke first. "Beck, you're a liar. You're a Jew like us. Otherwise, you wouldn't be in this camp."

"What I said was true, Lev. I was born in Bavaria, in a small town there. Füssen. A beautiful place. Rolling green hills in the spring and summer and pure white snow in the winter. A clear, lovely river, the Lech, and beautiful lakes. The water is sweet and pure. I was baptized a Catholic, but I never bothered with any of that."

"But your uniform has the yellow star like us."

"I suppose that's all that was available."

"Still, they should have placed you in some other camp. The ones for dissidents and criminals. Especially with you being a gentile. We don't want you here."

"I understand, Lev. But it's okay that I'm here. I am not a Jew, but I believe in your Jewish God. He's mine, too."

"Unlikely, Beck. I doubt you know our God. Are you a homosexual like they said?"

"I am not. But I am a pacifist, which to the Nazis is probably much worse. But it is good that we talk. What about you, Lev? Where were you born?"

"Me? Cottbus. But my parents were not German. They were Polish and Slavic. But I am a German by birth. And of course, a Jew."

"You must know the Sorbian language?"

"I do. But I haven't spoken it for years. How do you know that?"

"Because of Cottbus, where you were born. I'm a linguist, a student of languages. I know many languages. I was a professional document examiner and translator in Berlin. I even got to learn Arabic. But when I was processed following my conviction, I lied to them. I told them that, besides German, I only knew French and Polish. That way they would not use me for their war efforts. People who understand Polish and French as well as the German tongue are everywhere. Less so people who can translate Arabic and other foreign languages."

"I see."

"Yes. It seems that each of us must be here because we have some skill, some background or education that the Nazis believe may be useful. Obviously, not skills in such great demand as to remove us from … this." Beck swept his hand before him. "But some sort of skill, nevertheless. Has any man here been sent to work in the factories or farms before?"

Silence.

"Then that is why they bother to keep us alive … barely. And it's why we must learn about each other. Our names, hometowns, occupations, skills, education. We will commit this knowledge to memory. We will get to know each other's faces. We will no longer be anonymous prisoners, mere numbers tattooed onto the arm. We will be men, the men we are supposed to be. Men who have identities and skills and hometowns and loved ones. When we know ourselves and understand that our lives have purpose and value, we survive. We work for each other. We effect an escape. And then we walk out of here as free men."

With that the electric lights were extinguished. They heard footsteps and then someone banging on the locked door. "Lights out! No more speaking! Sleep!"

…

But sleep in the camp for anyone was nearly impossible. Over and over, the prisoners heard the sounds of overhead Allied aircraft. And then the bombs. The explosions blasted the ground. Levinsky felt his body tingle with the vibrations of the earth. He figured that the target was likely the nearby railway station. *Very close. Maybe we're next?*

…

Dawn finally broke. Hammel and Bauer found their way over to the large mess hall. The room felt enormous. They were alone. Bauer figured that at some point four hundred or more troops must have dined within the four walls.

Breakfast was not too bad. Lukewarm, lumpy oatmeal and coffee. At least the coffee was hot. The food and coffee had been brought in to them by an old Polish woman from the kitchen adjoining the dining hall.

Hammel spoke. "What do you make of this, Bauer? Why so empty? Where are all the other men?"

"I don't know. Probably all the bombings. There are rumors that the Americans are moving this way. Possibly Russians. But it has to be just talk, or they wouldn't have brought us here. They'd have evacuated us, too, right? Otherwise, it wouldn't make sense."

Sergeant Wittmer and Corporal Emmerich entered the room. They had already eaten breakfast in the formal dining hall with Lieutenant Magnus. Fried eggs, ham slices, and French bread.

Hammel and Bauer immediately stood to attention and saluted. "Heil!"

Emmerich returned the salute. "Heil, men. Hammel, round up two or three healthy Jews to shovel out the latrine trenches at B barracks."

"Yes sir. But I don't know if there are even three able-bodied Jews available."

"Well, find one or two, and then you too will shovel with them. Or get three, and you become their guard. Your choice. Understood?"

"Yes sir. May I finish eating?"

Emmerich shrugged. "I don't care. Just make sure it gets done! Bauer, go with him. Be thankful that it's only the trenches and not the big pit!"

"Yes sir!"

...

"Young soldier, you say you want me, the queer, and one other man here to shovel shit? Okay. Can you feed us first?" Levinsky scowled.

"No! Assemble yourselves and follow me to the back at the trenches! Right now. And bring those full buckets with you!"

Levinsky looked over to Beck who was sitting against the wall. "Get up, Beck. Time to shovel shit. We need one more. Can any of you stand?"

A few men shakily raised themselves to their feet.

"Lev, these men are still too weak to help us. Maybe in a few days they could when they'll be stronger. We'll tell the German boy that we'll do the work of three."

Levinsky scoffed. "Certainly, Beck. I'll do my third of the digging. You can dig the rest."

…

Hammel watched Levinsky and Beck make their way to the trenches. "Only two? I said three!"

Beck spoke. "Young Hammel, we are feeling fit today and will accomplish the work of three. You needn't worry. Right Mr. Levinsky?"

Levinsky scowled and grumbled.

Hammel pointed to a latrine pit several yards beyond the building. "Dump that shit over there in the old pit. And then grab those shovels and start digging out the latrines here!"

The ground was soft enough to shovel, a consequence of the first frost having not yet arrived. The men moved shovelfuls of filth into a warped, rusted wheelbarrow.

Bauer held his nose. "My God, the stench!" He moved back several paces and grabbed two wooden crates. "Here, Hammel, have a seat."

"I'll stand!" Hammel stood, gripping his short, stubby club.

Levinsky said something in a foreign tongue. "Okay, Mr. Linguist. What did I just say?"

Beck laughed. "Well, pretty funny, actually."

"Oh? You think I just told you a joke?"

Beck shook his head. "No, no. I mean funny like ironic, because I'm a pacifist. You quoted from the Torah in Hebrew. Deuteronomy. 'Vengeance is mine and I will repay them. In time their foot will slip, for the day of their disaster is at hand.' A famous quote of our Lord God."

"*Our* Lord God? I think not Beck. You're a goy. But yes. So you do know a little Hebrew. Many goyim do."

"Here's one I like better. And, yes, my Hebrew is a little rusty." Beck began speaking in Hebrew. "'And if a stranger dwells with you in your land, you shall not mistreat him. The stranger shall be to you as one born among you, and you shall love him as yourself, for you were once strangers in the land of Egypt.'"

"Not bad, Beck. Maybe a little too scholarly in your pronunciations. But not bad. Now shovel harder because I have almost completed my third."

Hammel slapped his club against his palm. "You two. Stop speaking Jew. It is forbidden. German only!"

Beck stopped shoveling and looked beyond Hammel and Bauer into the distance. He smiled and waved his hand. Hammel and Bauer instinctively looked over their shoulders to see who Beck was waving to. *No one.* They quickly looked back.

"Keep shoveling!"

"Certainly, young Hammel. And, you know you shouldn't be concerned. We were just quoting from the Bible. Being a Catholic, I'm sure you have no quarrel with the Bible."

"No Christian has a quarrel with the Bible, idiot."

"Of course. Although, I sometimes think the Nazis must have some quarrel with us, even though we read the same Bible. We Catholics, that is. I am a Catholic, too. You probably are aware of the persecution of Catholics going on within the Reich. I would be cautious if I were you. They show great favor to the Protestants. You know the Führer wants to establish a uniform Nazi religion made up from the different Protestant sects. Catholics excluded, of course."

"That is not my business and certainly not yours, queer."

"Yes. I only mention it because it is unfair to the Catholics who faithfully follow the laws and duties of the Third Reich. I presume they know you are a Catholic because of how they treat you. Very unfairly. You should be treated as their equal but never are."

"Why do you think I am a Catholic, queer?"

"Young Hammel, call me Beck or Otto, my given name. The name my loving parents gave me at birth. I'm not actually a queer, though. You may call me 'pacifist' if you want. That is accurate and true. But to answer your question, I knew many Hammels growing up in my village in Bavaria. Classmates and friends. Their parents were friends of my parents. The Hammels were all Catholics. Every single one. The Hammels have kind hearts. All of them. Utterly generous and kind to a fault. Each one would give the shirt off their back. The most kind and loving people I knew. And all Catholic."

Beck took a break from shoveling and looked up to Hammel. "Just like you, young Hammel. I can tell you, too, have a good heart. And your parents too, I am certain." Beck went back to shoveling. "And I'm just as certain that your parents are heartbroken now, without their son. Especially in light of the persecutions suffered by Catholics everywhere. I'm sure they worry greatly about you. They cry in their sleep, praying that you will return to them safely. That you may all be reunited back home to do good deeds and help them and other Catholics who are persecuted. To take care of each other, as a good son would do, to love and protect his parents. To save them from persecution."

Levinsky had been watching Hammel's face. He saw tears flow gently from the boy's eyes.

Beck continued shoveling. "Fortunately, you are here as a volunteer. Not conscripted. Because you are too young to serve. Yes, young men, motivated to do good for their country, sometimes lie about their age. But, of course, such young men are free to leave their voluntary service at will. In fact, the German authorities, in finding out about such an underage volunteer, would immediately discharge such person from service. Because the laws of the Reich require such. It is unlawful for an underage man to serve. A very important law."

Hammel quickly wiped away his tears, careful to hide the action of his wrist against his face. "I know nothing of that. I am a soldier just like anyone else. And I don't care about these religious things, Beck. None of that concerns me. Only my duties to the Reich."

"Of course, of course. Just making conversation."

…

Emmerich inspected the work. "Poor work, Hammel. Deficient. Barely deep enough. Grab a shovel and dig about six inches deeper."

"Can I get the Jews to do it?"

"No, Hammel. You do it. Now."

"May I help him, sir?"

"Bauer? Sure. If you feel inclined to shovel shit this morning, suit yourself. Tomorrow you'll be shoveling ours."

…

Levinsky sat against the wall next to Beck. They had finally been fed. Hammel and Bauer had removed the gruel and water barrels minutes before.

"Why were you torturing the boy earlier, Beck? Hammel is just a child."

"I wish him no harm, Lev. I just wanted him to think of his parents again. To see things through different eyes. To know that his parents still love him and want him back. That he has certain freedoms to exercise."

"That's great, Beck, but if he leaves here, he'll be hunted down and shot like a rabid dog. That's why your God is not my God. At least I don't want the boy to die."

"Well, I doubt very much that these Nazis would bother to mount a search for him. How many German soldiers are even in this camp? Far too few to send off to track down a child who shouldn't even be here."

"How do you know that? Who knows how many Nazi pigs are coming and going in and out of this camp."

"Well, we've seen only the two young privates and the two SS officers, Emmerich the corporal, and Wittmer the sergeant. And we saw the lieutenant who called himself Magnus when we passed through the gate. The lieutenant mentioned a colonel when we first arrived. But we've never seen him. How many more could there be?"

"What difference? There could be only one German soldier. But as long as he's holding a rifle, it may as well be a squadron."

"True, Lev. True. But having fewer German soldiers works well with the plan."

"Plan? Of course, Beck. Go shit yourself." Levinsky paused, waiting for a retort. There was none. "By the way, how did you know the boy was Catholic? Do you even know any Hammels?"

"I guessed he was Catholic because he had carved IHS into his club, a Catholic monogram for Jesus. And, no, I've never met any Hammels before."

...

The morning passed quickly. Many of the men were exhausted due to lack of sleep the night before and slept following breakfast. By midday, most had awoken. Beck broke the silence. "Today, we'll start to learn everyone's name and background. I'll go first. I am Otto Beck from the village of Füssen in Bavaria. I am twenty-six years old. I'm a professional linguist, translator, and document examiner. I worked for private companies as well as the government in Berlin. I was married but lost my wife and child several years ago."

Levinsky spoke. "I'm sorry to hear of that, Beck. Because of the war?"

"No, Lev. Both through childbirth. It has its dangers. I never got to know my son, and I miss my wife so greatly. But it opened my eyes. I realized that some things can't be changed. They just happen. But I also found hope in knowing of all the things that I *could* change. There are so many things that we can do. Ways to change each other's lives for the better. A universe of things."

Beck looked over to the man sitting to his right. "How about you, sir."

The frail man cleared his throat. "I am Eli Goldenberg. A watchmaker. Well, more of a watch and clock repairman. I was getting a little too old to build the watches that I built in my younger day. Repairs mostly. I am fifty-two years old. I was born in Berlin. I have a wife, two boys, and six grandchildren. I lost touch with them all when they rounded up all the men in the village. I think and pray for them, constantly."

"Yes. Thinking and praying is the best that we can do. Nice to meet you, Eli." Beck extended his hand, and Goldenberg grasped it gingerly, returning the greeting.

"May I go next?"

Beck looked over to another prisoner who leaned against the cold woodstove. "Of course, sir."

"I am Morris Schenk. From Kaiserslautern. A German Jew. Thirty-eight. Divorced. One daughter. They both emigrated to America years ago before it got bad. I was an engineer. Motors, mostly electric car motors. But now they're all gasoline and diesel, so I then did mechanical work. In a factory. On other kinds of electric motors."

"That's good, Morris. But don't forget, you *are* an engineer. Not, you *were* an engineer."

"Certainly. Very little engineering going on in here, Beck. But certainly."

"Ha. Yes. How about you, Lev? Would you take a turn?"

Levinsky scowled. "If I must. Isadore Levinsky. Jew. That's why I'm here."

"Okay, Lev. Wife? Family?"

"This is ridiculous, Beck. We are all dead men. No one cares who we are or were."

Beck looked around to the glum faces. "We care. Right, men? Morris, Eli?"

Levinsky saw most of the men nodding. Goldenberg responded, "I would like to hear, Lev."

Levinsky sighed. "Okay. I am thirty. From Cottbus. My wife and only son left me, but we are not divorced. I cheated. Took up with a woman. She's dead now. Gunned down in the street. I was a teacher and school principal. I taught boys and young men, all grades. Ran several schools as administrator. The Nazis put me to work teaching the children of the officers serving in some of the larger camps. Everything was fine until one young officer named Lindauer claimed that I had scowled at him. Scowled. He thought it showed disrespect. So he sent me into the general population. And now I am here."

Beck smiled. "Well, I find it hard to believe that you scowled, Lev."

The men began laughing.

"Very funny, Beck! Yes, I scowl. It suits my disposition. Just as your smile suits that of an idiot!"

Beck chuckled. "Yes, yes! I earned that. I can't help that I like to smile, and you can't help the scowling. So we're even."

The men heard the sounds of the barracks door being unlocked. It swung open and banged against the wall. Emmerich walked in holding a cowhide satchel accompanied by Bauer who pointed his rifle at the prisoners. Hammel followed behind with a chipped porcelain bowl filled with water. Emmerich placed his bag on the ground, pulled a straight razor out of his pocket and opened it.

"Time to shear the flock. Sit down in two lines before me!"

He watched the men slowly take their places. He removed a stained white towel and cracked hand mirror from his satchel. "One man at a time gets the razor. Scalps and faces. Use the water. Don't use the razor against your fellow Jew or you will be shot. Finish, dry yourself, and pass the razor to the next Jew. Hammel, if any Jew can't manage, you do it for them."

"Why do I have to touch a Jew? They're filthy."

"Because that is your job, Hammel. If you catch some lice, so what. Everyone gets lice. We'll delouse you with the Jews!"

Emmerich stood, watching the men painfully shave their scalps and faces with the worn straight razor. He laughed loudly each time a man cried out in pain from a razor cut. He pointed. "Look at all the blood, Hammel! Hey, Jew, you missed a spot!"

Having enjoyed his sport, Emmerich left the barracks.

Beck spoke up. "Private Bauer, will we be provided an opportunity to shower? Many of us haven't bathed in some time."

"It's broken, Beck. Maybe later when it's fixed."

Hammel added, "Yes, hopefully when it's nice and cold outside for you Jews."

The shaving exercise was completed. The men sat around feeling their bleeding cuts on their scalps, faces, and even hands. Beck looked around at his fellow sufferers. *Best to let everyone be for now.*

. . .

"Let's feed the Jews now, Hammel. Then we can enjoy our dinners."

"Why, Bauer? We come first."

"Yes. I just thought it may be better for … us to get it out of the way."

"Okay, Bauer. If you want."

The two unlocked the barracks and dragged the barrels inside. Bauer spoke. "Feeding time, prisoners. Line up." He looked over to the sullen men. Some had pulled off bits of thread from their tattered uniforms to staunch the bleeding of their cuts.

Afterward, he and Hammel dined alone in the massive mess hall. Beans, a sole piece of bread and coffee, just as the night before.

"I saw something today, Hammel. Those three large buildings by the hill and near the forest? The signs say those are munitions factories. They're all locked up now. No workers."

"So?"

"Well, what kinds of places do enemy bombers hit?"

"Factories, but how would they know where?"

"I don't know, Hammel. They seem to have some idea where they want to bomb. The problem is, if they want to bomb those buildings, our quarters are not really all that far away. Bombing is not an exact science. They just drop a bunch in a general area and hope for some hits. That may be why the bombing is getting closer."

...

The lights went out in the barracks, but there would be no sleep for the prisoners. The sound of Allied aircraft rumbled throughout the atmosphere. Almost immediately they heard violent explosions causing the earth to tremble. Several men began to moan in fear. Levinsky murmured: "Good God, they're even closer tonight."

Moments later, another bomb struck. The frame of the building shook as the sound of the explosion blasted through the air. Several prisoners cried out. Levinsky cried out too. "God in heaven!"

Just as quickly, the sounds of aircraft subsided. The men shook with fear, waiting for the telltale sounds of a second bombing run.

"Beck, what do you think? Ready to meet your maker?"

"Not really, Lev. Not yet, I hope!"

"I know you gentiles think there's an afterlife. Ours isn't until the end when the dead are resurrected. Or at least that's what my people have said. But you goyim are sent to either heaven or hell, right? So you're all afraid of going to hell."

"Well, that's what they say. For me, I found a workaround."

"Of course, Beck. Of course you would! Pray tell!"

"Well, I figure that most people want to go to heaven as their big reward. You know, they worked hard and did good deeds and worshipped in their church and all that. And then, once dead, they can just relax in heaven. No more worries, no toils, no conflicts. But even before I am judged, I will make it very clear to God that He should take into account that I am very willing to work. I don't want to laze about somewhere in heaven or crumple up and suffer eternally in hell. I want to work. Whatever He wants. No job too small or too big. I'll do it happily. Maybe He'll want me to help somebody down here? Maybe take away some of their load? Who knows. But my willingness to work—and to work hard—will keep me out of hell. What do you think?"

"Most unlikely, Beck. Most unlikely. But great nonsense. I would have expected nothing less."

Levinsky had barely completed his sentence when the droning sounds of aircraft began to accelerate in volume. *Even closer sounding.* Moments later, a terrifying explosion battered the ground just outside the camp. Instinctively, nearly every man cried out in terror.

"Better pray to your Catholic God, Beck."

…

At daybreak, Magnus, Wittmer and Emmerich met to check for possible damage. They made their way to the factory buildings.

Magnus spoke. "Close. Very close. Look at the size of the crater, just outside the fence on the hill."

Wittmer pointed to the building closest to the hill. "Look, sir. Part of the wall has caved in from the vibration."

They walked over. Magnus sighed. "Not good. That's going to require substantial reconstruction. But, even if we could find a few Jews strong enough to do it, at present, we have no access to suitable building materials. Supply lines are stalled. All we can do is request supplies and wait."

Emmerich nodded. "Sir, if the colonel is available today, would you like me to accompany the colonel here, so that I can show him the damage while you request building materials?"

"That won't be necessary, Corporal. I'll inform the colonel momentarily and accompany him here should he desire an inspection."

"Yes sir."

. . .

Hammel and Bauer sat glumly in the mess hall. Breakfast had arrived. Oatmeal and coffee.

Hammel shook his head. "They used to feed us scrapple and eggs. I don't even like oatmeal."

"I know. But you have to eat it. It's all we get." Bauer stopped chewing and took a sip of coffee. Lukewarm. "I saw that you didn't sleep either. The bombs were very nearly exploding in this camp. I bet they were aiming for those three buildings."

"Let's look, and then we'll feed the Jews."

Emmerich and Wittmer entered the mess hall. Hammel and Bauer immediately stood and saluted. "Heil!"

Emmerich pointed. "Both of you will dig out a fresh latrine pit by our quarters. Come now."

The two followed behind Emmerich. He pointed to the precise area and gave specifications for the task. "Dig a five-by-five-foot square area to a depth of three feet. That shouldn't be too hard to accomplish."

"Sir, should we feed the prisoners first?"

"No, Bauer. After. Do my bidding first."

"Yes sir."

. . .

Daylight found the prisoners demoralized and afraid. Levinsky grumbled out loud. "Will they ever feed us?"

The prisoners grumbled back in return. Several touched at their cuts from the day before. Still sore.

Beck stood. "I know we're all tired from lack of sleep. And hungry too. But let's distract ourselves by picking up where we left off yesterday. Would anyone like to take a turn?"

Levinsky scowled and shook his head. "Give it a rest, Beck."

One man raised his hand. "I will. I'll speak. I am Issac Cohen from Stralsund. Sixty-two years old. Cartographer. I make maps, or at least I did until my eyesight began to worsen. I can see well enough for most things, but not the small details anymore. I'm a widower. My wife and I adopted two children, a boy and girl, adults now. They both live in Spain. I haven't been in contact with them for a long time because of … this." He waved his hand in the air.

"Spain sounds pleasant, Issac. Have you visited there?"

"Many times, Beck. They live in the same southern region, but different towns. Very nice there." He thought back to the warm breezes from the ocean in summer.

"Sounds wonderful, Issac. When we are all free, please send our greetings to them when you next visit."

Cohen smiled. "Yes. Yes. I will certainly!"

Levinsky shook his head and grumbled.

"Who's next?"

"Me. Sol Ephraim. I'm forty-eight. From Schwerin. But I'm just a bookkeeper. I worked for a local bank. I'm not a full accountant, so I don't know if being a bookkeeper is what's kept me away from factory work."

"Well, just working at a bank … being trustworthy. You're probably here for that as much as bookkeeping. But tell us more. Are you married?"

"Yes, and two daughters, twenty-three and twenty-six. But I don't know what's happened to them. Same as Mr. Goldenberg. I guess we pray. What else is there to do?"

…

"I don't think this is going to be deep enough, Bauer. The corporal wanted three feet. It looks barely two."

"Well, my arms are getting tired, Hammel. And I'm already hungry for lunch, and we haven't even fed the Jews yet. They're probably starving. Let's stop and let Emmerich tell us if it needs to be deeper."

"Who cares about the Jews, Bauer? They will all die soon enough as our Führer has decreed."

"True. But even farm animals need to be fed and watered. Just because we exploit the farm animal for what it provides us, doesn't mean that we should make the animal suffer too. We should treat the Jews at least as well as animals we use."

"I think this is different, Bauer, because of the laws now in place against them."

Bauer sighed. "Still, when you were a boy, were you cruel to your dog or cat? Did you deliberately torment your pet?"

"Of course not. But I didn't have a cat. Just a dog." Hammel thought back to Wilhelm. He hadn't realized how much he would miss the dog. He didn't think about things like that when he volunteered for the Army after serving in the Hitler Youth. But he thought of Wilhelm a lot at night, especially during the bombings. He thought about his parents even more. Especially last night.

"Well, I don't think that Emmerich has been treating the Jews properly, Hammel. They are prisoners. They're not going anywhere. Why torment and taunt them like he does? Why delay their feeding? This is not a death camp, so the prisoners are supposed to be kept alive, not slowly killed."

"That is not our business, Bauer. And I would not speak like that again if I were you. Corporal Emmerich is our superior officer."

"Yes, but don't forget that I'm a senior private. Just a notch below corporal. A small notch."

"Yes, Bauer, but he and the rest are SS. We are just regular army. Didn't you want to join the SS?

"No, Hammel. I was drafted when I turned eighteen. I had no desire to join the SS. I am a member of the Nazi party only because my father desired it."

"I would have joined the SS, but I volunteered for the army."

"Hammel, you are actually not even a soldier. Do you realize that? Were you issued a gun? Do you have military ID? No. You do not. You are a good young man, but you don't belong here."

"That's a lie, Bauer! I enlisted!"

"Impossible. You are not eighteen. You remind me of my baby brother … very much in fact. He is twelve years old. I would guess you are about thirteen."

"Age doesn't matter when one fights for the Fatherland!"

"Perhaps twelve?"

Hammel had become red-faced and flustered. "I'm going on thirteen, Bauer. In one month. Not twelve!"

…

Hammel and Bauer unlocked the barracks door and dragged the two barrels inside.

Hammel barked, "Same as before. Line up."

"Thank you, young Hammel and Bauer. We were talking about the lives we led before our imprisonment. May we continue to converse with each other while we eat and drink?"

"No! Don't speak!"

"Okay, Hammel. We won't." Beck took his place at the end of the line. "It's interesting, though, how varied our lives have been. Even though we are all here in this place at this very time, we've all lived very different lives. Of course, the Army High Command has all of this information about us."

Hammel smirked. "Our High Command? Why would that be?"

"Well, I suppose the colonel didn't tell you, but each of us is here because of the special skills we possess. Skills that could be useful to the Reich. I had presumed that the colonel would have mentioned it to you by now. My apologies."

Bauer spoke. "You presume to know the colonel now, Beck?"

"No, of course not, Bauer. Besides a friendly wave the other day when digging the latrines, I haven't seen him about. And he definitely has not visited us here in the barracks. If someone says he has, ignore it."

Hammel looked over to Bauer, inquisitively. "I've never seen the colonel."

Bauer shrugged. "Don't listen to them, Hammel. Be quiet, Beck. Prisoners, just eat and take your water."

...

"Deficient. Dig it two feet deeper. Then, as punishment, there's bootblacking to be done. The sergeant and I will leave our boots outside our doors. You will find shoe polish and brushes in your own quarters. Use them. Shine to SS specifications, not regular army. Then take your lunch."

Hammel watched Emmerich walk away. "I told you it wasn't deep enough."

Bauer sighed. "The bastard. Okay, more digging and bootblacking. But what else would we do today? Patrol. And patrol some more. Walks around the perimeter for no reason. Besides feeding and taking the Jews out to the latrine, patrolling is all we've done here."

"Better than bootblacking."

"Maybe. Have you noticed that no supply trucks have come through the gates since we've been here? And no one mans the gates. I watched the Polish women workers just open the gate for themselves on the way out. They get picked up by a civilian auto. I guess they live in the town."

Hammel shook his head. "Who cares. Guard duty at the gate would be even worse punishment than bootblacking."

…

Levinsky spoke for all to hear. "That's clever, Beck. Trying to trick the children into thinking you're a good friend of the colonel. What does that get us?"

"Admittedly, nothing for now. But it's what we 'anarchists' do. Spread confusion."

Several of the men chuckled.

"Fine, Beck. Waste your time and vocal cords any way you want."

"Come now, Lev. Confusion is an important element in our plan. It's one of the few arrows we have in our quiver."

"Spoken like a true pacifist."

Beck laughed. "Yes. Very good, Lev. But my arrow is not pointed and cannot harm a man's body. Perhaps his mind, though. Now, let's continue introducing ourselves. Who would like a turn?"

Slowly a man raised his arm. "I do. Heinz Gelbach from Leipzig. I'm fifty-eight. I'm married with two sons. Both were sent to work camps. But my wife, last time I heard, was alive and living with her sister in France on a farm. She bribed some men and crossed the border. A month later, the Nazis had taken France. But I heard that she and her sister are safe."

"That's encouraging, Heinz. What is your occupation?"

"I'm an airplane pilot. But I only know the single-engine, small planes. I did crop dusting. I've never been inside a military plane."

"Still, being a pilot is a great skill. That must be why you're here. I'm surprised the Nazis didn't place you into the skilled work force."

"Well, I think I know why they didn't. My pilot's license was revoked before I was seized. I had one or two small accidents, you see. If you want a pilot that can fly a single-engine plane into a windmill, I am that man."

The men laughed.

"Very good, Heinz. Who else would like a turn."

A man with particularly bad razor cuts on his scalp raised his hand. "Elias Matzner. I'm forty-two, from Hannover. I am a telegraph repairman. I was married but encouraged my wife to divorce me for her own safety because she was not a Jew. She did. We have a daughter and I do not know her whereabouts."

Matzner began sobbing, gently. He collected himself, quickly, and inhaled deeply. "Sorry, sorry. So much sadness."

"Yes, Elias, yes. We all feel as you do. Did you enjoy your work?"

"It was a trade. I was a master technician, but with all the telephones, suddenly the telegraph was not as important. So repairman was all I could be."

"Yes. But that's still a valuable trade. Especially at wartime."

Matzner nodded.

"May I go next?"

"Of course!"

"Hirsch Wenig. I'm forty-nine, a widower. No living children due to pneumonia. My career may surprise you. I was a corporal in the Army. I was chief assistant to the procurement officer. I learned about barter and trade with suppliers, farmers, meatpackers, bakers, manufacturers and so on. Yes, I served my country proudly until

Jews were no longer permitted to serve. And this is my reward. Now I serve my country locked up in a camp."

"But not for long, Hirsch. Not for long."

…

By late afternoon, each man had taken the opportunity to introduce himself. Some realized that they knew some of the same people from the past, through careers, education, or geography. The volume of conversation in the barracks increased greatly as the men got to know each other better. Beck was happy to hear the occasional sound of laughter among the men. He joined in the conversations to learn the birthdates of each man.

As dusk fell, the conversation began to wane. Bauer and Hammel delivered the usual meal of gruel and water. After eating, the men rested.

Beck spoke. "Men, it pleases me that we've all conversed together today. This is precisely how we win, how we achieve victory and walk out of here as free men."

Levinsky growled. "Victory? Free men? Unlikely, Beck. Most unlikely. Look around. We are all still here, still prisoners. Miserable prisoners. Talking with one another hasn't gotten us anywhere. None of us have wished our way out of here. You've been the happy ringmaster, but you haven't yet told us the important part. Your plan, Beck. Tell us, in detail, about your big plan for our escape."

"Lev, I think it best I keep the workings of the plan to myself, as there is some fluidity involved."

"Ha! Of course. More nonsense! You are cruel, Beck. Giving these men false hope. Men, if you haven't figured it out already, Beck is a liar. Not one word of truth has fallen from his glib lips since we've been here!"

"Lev, in my own defense, yes, I have told many lies to the Nazis. Because such advances the plan. But as far as you and the rest of our men are concerned, most of what I say is reasonably truthful."

"'Reasonably truthful?' More nonsense! Stop giving us false hope, Beck. We don't need it!"

The men sat in absolute silence. They listened to the sound of their own breathing. An eternity seemed to pass. Finally, Goldenberg spoke. "I like having hope. Hope of any kind—true, false … it doesn't matter. I know that we are all likely to die here. We all know that. But, for me, please continue with hope, Beck."

The rest of the men began murmuring in agreement. The murmuring grew louder with several prisoners thanking Beck.

"I'll do what I can, men. And Lev, may I note one correction. I never said that our goal was to escape from here. Escape is not for us."

Stunned silence overwhelmed the barracks.

"A prisoner who escapes carries his prison with him, forever. He's a wanted man, hunted until death or recapture. We won't have that."

Lev growled, "Listen, Beck, I'm certain, and these men are certain, that you told us you had an escape plan!"

"That's correct, Lev. But escape is not for us. Escape is for the Nazis. We're going to help each Nazi in this camp escape. And then we'll leave here as free men."

…

Bauer and Hammel sat together in the lonely mess hall. Finally, one of the old Polish women brought them plates of lukewarm beans and two small loaves of rock-hard, stale bread.

"This meal is even worse than yesterday's."

"I know, Hammel. And the oatmeal they feed us in the morning is barely better than the gruel they feed the prisoners. I patrolled past the officer's dining hall earlier today before dinnertime. They are feeding the SS men roasted meats, cheeses, and even fruit. Pies, too! Wonderful smells. And I bet their bread isn't stale."

"It's not fair."

"No, it's not. And that's why you will leave here at dusk. You will head back to your family. They need you, and I'm sure they miss you."

"Never, Bauer! I am not a deserter!"

"That's correct, Hammel. You can't be a deserter if you are not a soldier. You are a volunteer."

"I told you before, Bauer, I enlisted. I am a soldier, just like you!"

Bauer paused as he tried to gnaw through his loaf of bread. "Okay, then, soldier. As your superior, I order you to leave tonight."

"You can't do that, Bauer! You're no officer!"

"But I outrank you. Listen, Hammel, those Allied bombers will be back this evening. You see that the gates are unguarded. It's very likely that French Resistance fighters wander in here at night to locate structures for the Allied bombers. Like those factory plants. Like our barracks. The Allies want to kill as many German soldiers as possible. Barracks make a great target. Remember we are in Alsace, not Munich. The French are everywhere."

"I'm not afraid to give my life to the Fatherland!"

"Okay. Are you willing to be maimed for the Fatherland? To go about town as a cripple, unable to work, unable to take care of your parents in their old age? Not every enemy attack ends in a noble death. In the real world, men who do not die often return as useless cripples, begging for handouts. Without a wife or family. Because who would have a cripple?"

Hammel stopped eating and began to weep, gently.

"Then it's settled. You will be leaving here as a soldier with your head held proudly because you are following a superior's orders. After we feed the Jews, we will prepare your journey. I have money to give you. You'll dress in your civilian clothes, otherwise a Resistance sniper may take you down. You'll walk back toward the railroad station at dusk. But you are not to take the train. Trains and rail lines are targets. You will continue past the station to the road that leads to the village. There you will seek out a driver for hire who will take you back to your home by auto."

...

The prisoners fell into quiet conversations. Several of the men talked about sports, particularly boxing. Beck was surprised to hear the door suddenly unlatched and opened.

Bauer walked through. "I tried to procure the table scraps for you, but the old woman had shaken them out for the birds. I was able to take these two loaves of bread because the woman had thrown them in the garbage. I'm sure it's because they are very stale. But, if you want them, they are yours."

"Thank you, Private Bauer, thank you! We are very grateful for your kindness!"

"You're welcome, Beck. And please don't mention this to the officers."

"Of course not!"

After Bauer left, Beck handed a loaf to Levinsky. "Tough as nails, Lev. Do your best to break it up. I'll do this one."

As the men chewed, happily, through their stale chunks of bread, Beck remarked, "See, the plan is working!"

...

The night brought forth new terrors. Bauer laid on his cot listening to the rumbling sounds of the aircraft followed by enormous explosions. Much as one can detect the force of thunder by intensity of the preceding lightning, Bauer had become proficient in guessing the extent to which aircraft sounds would result in nearby destruction. Unable to sleep, he thought about Hammel, who he'd grown to think of as a little brother. He felt gratified knowing Hammel would be safe. *The bombers would not harm a village filled with civilians.*

Then he heard a particularly loud aircraft. Instinctively, he jumped out of his cot, grabbed his coat and ran outside the barracks and toward the dining hall. He felt the deafening sound of a tremendous explosion somewhere near the manufacturing buildings. He covered his ringing ears, waiting for a second strike. But there was none.

…

Dawn broke, and Bauer sought out Emmerich. He saw Emmerich and Wittmer together and followed them over to the site of the loudest explosion.

"Heil Hitler."

"Heil, Bauer. You do not need to accompany us. We will assess the damage to the camp."

"Yes sir. But I wanted also to report that the volunteer, Hammel, is missing. I saw that he placed his uniform in his footlocker and must have left camp in his civilian clothes. Probably sometime last evening."

"Did he steal a rifle? Your rifle?"

"No sir. I have my rifle. And there were no other rifles for him to steal."

"Then that is all, Bauer. And next time be more prompt with your report. The sun has been up for some time now."

"Yes sir."

"Go feed the Jews. We will follow behind in a few minutes for barracks inspection."

"Yes sir."

After Bauer left, Emmerich inquired, "Should we report this to Magnus?"

"No. Leave it be. The boy should not have been serving with us. Too young. If we report, we bring scrutiny upon ourselves."

…

Bauer obtained the barrels from the Polish woman and dragged them into the barracks just as Emmerich and Wittmer arrived, following behind him.

"Prisoners, form the usual line."

Beck spoke from the back of the line. "Private Bauer, I see that young Hammel is not present today. I presume he received the evacuation order?"

"No talking, Beck!"

Wittmer barked angrily, "What is he saying? Is that the queer?"

"Yes sir. The queer."

Beck spoke up. "For the record, Sergeant, I was not convicted for being a sexual deviant. I was convicted for the crime of treason, the same as our beloved Führer."

With that, Wittmer pulled Beck out of the line by his collar and struck him in his face with an open hand, boxing Beck's ear. Beck cried out in pain and dropped to one knee, holding his stinging face and ringing ear with his palm.

"Impertinent queer! Now stand up. You spoke of an evacuation order. Who informed you of such an order?"

Beck stood tentatively, defensively. "I beg your pardon, sir. A mistake on my part. I saw that Hammel was absent and presumed that the colonel had passed the order along to Lieutenant Magnus for further implementation."

"The colonel?" Wittmer laughed gruffly. "You and the colonel now speak regularly about camp administration? And when exactly did you see the colonel?"

"Again, my apologies sir. I haven't seen him for, perhaps a day or two. And for the record, he did not speak with me on camp matters. He made no such communication, besides a friendly wave while passing through the camp. The notion that the colonel passed along the order from Berlin to the lieutenant was mere speculation on my part. Whether the lieutenant received the order is unknown."

Wittmer shook his head and stared at Emmerich, angrily, who shook his head in response.

Beck spoke again. "And I know it's not my place to speculate, sir, but perhaps the lieutenant received but simply failed to share the order. With all the cavorting and such with the French woman, perhaps he was distracted?"

Emmerich barked, "What French woman?"

"Sorry, sir. I should not have repeated the rumor. We prisoners hear things. It's inevitable. These walls are porous. You can see daylight through the cracks." Beck pointed to the rays of sun piercing the ground through the wall. "And that's why, sometimes at night, we hear voices outside our barracks. The language is always French, though, usually whispered. I do know a very slight amount of French, but not the words I heard last time."

"What words did you hear?"

"I believe the words sounded something like … umm …ahh … 'usine.' And the other word I heard several times was 'cible, 'cible.' And then the word 'espionner.' But I don't know what any of those words mean. I am able to understand words like 'bonjour,' 'oui,' and 'non.'"

Wittmer walked over to Beck again and grabbed him by his sore ear, twisting it into his scalp. Beck fell to his knees and cried out in agony.

"Worthless queer! Tell me—at any time did you see Lieutenant with a French woman or any civilian?"

"No sir! I did not! Please accept my apologies. I should not have repeated rumors. Rumors are so often lies!"

Wittmer released his grip and pushed Beck down to the ground.

"Enough! Be quiet, queer! Bauer, when you have completed this task, see me in my quarters!"

Wittmer and Emmerich exited, slamming the barracks door behind them. Bauer walked over to Beck to help him up. "You sure know how to get everyone in trouble, Beck."

…

After Bauer left, the men surrounded Beck.

Goldenberg looked at Beck's ear. "Are you badly hurt, Beck?"

"Just a little sore, Eli. I'll be fine."

Levinsky scowled. "We're lucky he only smacked you. Those two Nazi pigs could have just as well shot you in the head and maybe the rest of us, too. If this is your 'plan,' Beck, I suggest you submit a new plan. Otherwise, you're going to get us all killed."

Heinz Gelbach spoke up. "So what, Levinsky. We are already dead men. At least we'd be going out making a little trouble. Who agrees?"

Every hand was raised, save Levinsky's. "Okay. If you men want to follow this pied piper off his cliff, go ahead. I can't stop you."

Beck finally spoke. "Lev is right. My plan does hold great risks for each of us. If anyone would prefer to stay behind when the rest of us walk out of here as free men, you certainly may do so. And by the way—one down and four to go."

Levinsky snarled. "What do you mean?"

"We helped Hammel escape. Now we have only four more left, not counting the mysterious, invisible colonel."

...

As ordered, Bauer went directly to the officers' residence to report to Wittmer. He saw Emmerich and Wittmer outside the residence smoking cigarettes.

Wittmer growled, "Are you aware of any evacuation order?"

"No sir."

"What about the queer. Has he met with the colonel? Have you seen them together?"

"No sir. But I once saw Beck wave to someone who Beck said was the colonel."

"You saw that?"

"Well, I saw Beck wave, but was unsure as to whether it was to the colonel or someone else. But I know he waved. Also, there was a rumor."

"What rumor?"

"About Beck meeting with the colonel in the barracks, but Beck firmly denied meeting with the colonel."

"But you believe they did meet?"

"No sir. I merely am reporting the rumor about the meeting."

"What was the source of this rumor?"

"Beck, sir."

"You are useless, Bauer. Let me ask you. Have you witnessed the lieutenant cavorting with the French woman?"

"No sir. And I'm not even sure which French woman."

"There have been more than one?"

"No. I mean I don't know, sir. I couldn't say how many there are."

"Very well. Patrol the camp thoroughly today. Should you see or encounter any signs of the French woman or any other civilian in this camp, report to me, immediately. Do not report to Lieutenant Magnus."

"Yes sir."

...

Calm had returned to B barracks. Several of the prisoners played games of tic-tac-toe scratched into the dirt floor, using straw to mark the sections. Others conversed quietly.

"Beck, when we were digging those latrines, you waved to someone. Who were you waving to?"

"To no one, Lev. I wanted to find out if Hammel and Bauer would turn around to see the person I was waving to. They did. While they turned, I also turned to get a look of the area behind us, to see as much of the camp as possible. I saw a dining hall, officers' residences, barracks, and some industrial buildings. I also saw that the gate wasn't guarded."

"You haven't heard any Frenchmen passing by this building at night, right? You were lying?"

"Yes, all lies."

"What were those French words?"

"The words were 'factory,' 'target,' and 'spy.' I suspect that Emmerich and Wittmer know exactly what those words mean."

"What about the colonel? You think there is no colonel here?"

"Think about it. No colonel was present when we arrived. No colonel has visited our barracks. The commanding officer at a prison camp always makes an initial inspection to make sure everyone knows who's in charge. To receive a fawning public display of obeisance from subordinates. To harass, threaten, and frighten prisoners. The fact that the mysterious colonel has not visited leads me to conclude that he's not here. The boy, Hammel, likewise said he hadn't seen the colonel. Something for us to exploit."

…

Lieutenant Magnus welcomed Wittmer and Emmerich to his luncheon table in the formal dining hall. "My apologies for missing breakfast with you this morning. I dined privately with the colonel in his quarters. Please fill me in on the damage."

As he spoke, one of the women workers came by serving steaming platters of sausages, boiled potatoes, and French bread.

Wittmer responded. "Indirect, but substantial, Lieutenant. The second munitions building was damaged, caved in from the effects of the bombing. The damage is worse than the damage to the third building that you observed yesterday."

"Unfortunate. And, sadly, there's not much we can do until supply lines are cleared and running again."

"Yes sir. Understood."

The conversation paused, awkwardly.

"And how is the colonel, sir?"

"In fine health, Sergeant. I will tell him you inquired."

"Thank you. There have been rumors about camp of an evacuation order in place, Lieutenant. But the colonel would have informed you of such, correct? Particularly since you breakfasted with him just hours ago?"

"The colonel mentioned no such order, Sergeant. And, yes, he certainly would have."

No further conversation ensued. Magnus was somewhat taken aback. Each meal so far had been quite collegial. Much enjoyable conversation. He wondered whether the two harbored suspicions about the colonel.

The three finished their lunches in near silence. Wittmer and Emmerich saluted respectfully and left.

…

"Emmerich, I think we need to consider the possibility that Lieutenant Magnus is a traitor. That Magnus has deliberately withheld knowledge of our evacuation order to advance his own goals, his own … desires."

"I agree, sir. If he has fallen under the influence of the French woman, or women, he will plan for his own safe exit to our detriment. He will abandon us to our own destruction."

"Yes. It seems probable that the colonel received an evacuation order perhaps only days before we arrived. The colonel obeyed the order effecting his own reassignment, while passing down implementation of the order for the rest of the company to Magnus. Magnus did not implement the order. Instead, he lied to our faces about the colonel, implying the colonel was present but simply unavailable. In reality, Magnus did so to prolong his stay at the camp, perhaps at the behest of the French. To help them identify buildings to bomb, including our residence. Perhaps to spend more time with the French woman, a likely spy."

"Yes. A sickening act of treachery. As for the boy, perhaps Magnus had enough of a conscience to inform the boy of the order and make sure he was safely evacuated."

"Yes."

"I think the only reasonable course of action for us is to track down the boy. Once we find him, we can confirm that he received an order to evacuate from Magnus. If that's the case, we'll communicate our findings to Berlin. Most importantly, and practically, there seems almost a certainty that the camp will face more bombing tonight. Our leaving the camp at dusk helps assure our survival and opportunity to report Magnus for treason."

"Agreed, Sergeant."

"Tonight, we pack our things just as though we received an order for reassignment and relocation. We commandeer the truck we came with. Do you recall the amount of fuel left in the tank?"

"Low, but probably enough to take us out of camp and to the village where we could re-fuel. I haven't found any fuel here in camp."

"Better than walking. And, for our own personal safety, I recommend we exit camp in our civilian clothes. The Resistance is likely sprinkled throughout these forests. Our German uniforms will expose us to peril. Particularly if we must make part of the journey on foot."

"Yes. A reasonable approach."

...

The day passed quickly for the prisoners. Beck devised a game whereby a prisoner was allotted points, represented by a piece of straw, for each item of information the prisoner could recall about another specified prisoner. Beck won, having memorized all information previously provided.

Bauer, as before, dragged the food and water barrels in for the men's dinners.

"Bauer, thanks again for bringing us the bread yesterday. But the men and I discussed it. We would prefer that you not expose yourself to risk in the future. If they catch you showing us mercy, there would certainly be consequences for you. Repercussions. We don't want that. We can survive with the food and water in the barrels. You need to be safe too. In fact, we would suggest that this evening, you bunk with us in these barracks. If the French Resistance has been about the camp, they will know that these barracks hold prisoners, not soldiers. On the other hand, your barracks could be targeted by bombers."

Bauer was both heartened and frightened by Beck's offer. "Well, thank you, Beck. But my duty lies with the Reich. I sleep in my own barracks. But I will take your advice about the extra food."

...

After Bauer left, Levinsky growled angrily. "Who gave you the right to turn down more food? Who gave you authority to invite the enemy here for his safety? I don't recall a vote! What new lies have you told, Beck?"

"You're right, Lev. I was lying to Bauer in some respects. Bauer is at great personal risk for showing us mercy. That's true. We don't want him to get in trouble. But I lied about the safety of these barracks. I doubt the Resistance would know or even care about a handful of nearly dead Germans. Yes, that's us, Lev. We're the Germans. German Jews and criminals. The Allies bomb Germans. But we very much need Bauer for the plan. We need him on our side, and we need him alive."

"Again, with the 'plan'! You refuse to reveal this plan, but if the plan requires us to assist our enemies, then I don't agree with this 'plan,' and I'm sure the other Jews here feel the same. Bad enough having one insufferable goy prisoner among us. God forbid we now have to house and protect enemy goyim, too."

"I'm sorry, Lev. And men. I perhaps should have mentioned Bauer's importance in advance. But I hope you keep faith in the plan. And again, any man who would like to work independently and outside of the plan may do so. Just let me know, and I will adjust the plan accordingly."

Sol Ephraim spoke. "I like the plan, Beck, and I don't even know what the hell it is. What I do know is that I would rather not sit here and rot away until death. If your plan even has a slight chance of success, I like your plan. The plan of rotting away here is not a good plan."

Most of the men murmured their agreement. Levinsky scowled.

...

Night fell to a nearly full moon. A tree falling in a forest may or may not make a sound. A truck stalling on a road running through a forest does. That evening, the forest outside the camp listened and also heard the precise and efficient gunfire of a sniper's rifle. The Resistance sharpshooter and spotter ran over to their felled prey. The two who had abandoned their truck to walk on foot were obvious targets. Civilian men wearing the gun belts and holsters of the SS. The identification papers seized from their dead bodies confirmed the kills. One corporal and one sergeant.

...

Later that evening came the bombers. Bauer shuddered upon hearing the sounds of the aircraft. Louder than any before. He knew the aircraft and its bombs were very close. He had remained dressed in his uniform. He didn't want to run out in his long johns and coat as he had the night before. He grabbed his coat and ran out of his barracks toward the dining hall, away from the three manufacturing buildings. He heard the intense rumbling of the Allied bomber overhead and crouched against the wall.

The noise from the explosions set his ears ringing. The impact produced a manmade earthquake that nearly knocked him over. He felt certain that the bombs had taken out some or all of the buildings. He waited in the cold for more aircraft sounds. He heard them, but more distant. He decided to stay away from his barracks for the remainder of the night. He did not sleep. He would not have been able to sleep in his barracks, either.

...

At daybreak, Lieutenant Magnus sought out Wittmer and Emmerich. He needed a damage assessment. He was greatly concerned for his own personal safety. He hoped that filing a comprehensive report about the persistent bombing and extensive damage would result in an evacuation. The camp was not a safe place to be. He entered the officers' residence and was surprised to discover that Wittmer and Emmerich were absent. Their barracks were stripped bare of all clothing, including their duffels. He felt nauseous. *Gone.*

He thought back to his conversation with the colonel, just a day before the new prisoners arrived. He'd promised the colonel that he would cover for him. He had no choice. The colonel had always looked out for him. He had to reciprocate, even though doing so exposed him to severe disciplinary action. If he was lucky, he would only be stripped of his rank and discharged from the SS and not thrown in prison. Now he was stuck covering up for the colonel's absence with a series of lies and obfuscations.

Why isn't he back yet? The colonel was days overdue. He hoped to God that the colonel had not deserted. *If he has, I'll be shot as an accomplice.*

As Magnus tried to collect his thoughts he heard a car horn sound in the distance. A car at the gate. He hurriedly jogged down to open the gate, hoping to see the colonel. He felt another wave of nausea. The car's occupant was Captain Gessert, not the colonel.

Magnus saluted formally and opened the gate. He watched the staff car rumble through, generously allowing Magnus to catch up on foot. They met in Magnus's office, just outside the colonel's.

Gessert sat tensely in the chair before the desk. "It's about time, Lieutenant. You left me waiting at the gate."

Magnus nearly threw himself into his office chair. He panted, "My apologies, Captain. We suffered another bombing last night, and I was reviewing the damage for the colonel."

"Very well. I'm here for the mandated prison inspection. I have many other camps and sub-camps to visit today and tomorrow, so time is of the essence. Where is the colonel?"

"I believe that he's in his office, but I think he mentioned that he's presently indisposed."

"Indisposed? Very well, if he wants to cloister himself in there this morning and deny me basic professional courtesies, that is his prerogative. And the prerogative of his rank. But I have a schedule to keep. I must undertake the prison inspection, immediately."

"Yes sir!"

As the two approached the B barracks, they observed Bauer dragging the barrels of gruel and water to the entrance door. Gessert barked, "Keep those outside, Private. I'm going to inspect the prisoners first."

Bauer saluted. "Heil Hitler. Yes, Captain."

The prisoners had been mostly standing around, stretching and conversing about the prior evening's bombing. They heard the familiar sound of the door being unlocked and watched as Gessert entered first, followed by Magnus and Bauer.

Gessert barked loudly, "Prisoners, sit down before me in two rows, hands on your heads." He watched as the men complied. "Are all prisoners accounted for, Private? What is the count?"

Bauer responded tersely. "Yes, Captain. All accounted for. The count is twenty-two."

As Gessert walked past the rows of men sitting below him, he heard a voice.

"Good morning, Captain! Very nice to see you today!"

Gessert looked up angrily. "Who spoke? Stand up immediately!"

Beck stood, still holding his hands to his head. "It was I, Captain. Prisoner Otto Beck. I wanted to welcome you to our barracks! Usually, we see Corporal Emmerich and Sergeant Wittmer. Presumably, they also received the evacuation order. That's probably why they are not present today."

"Be quiet, Jew!" Gessert looked over to Magnus. "What is this Jew speaking of? Was such an order issued?"

"No, Captain. There is no such order … to my knowledge!"

Gessert walked over to Beck. He unholstered his sidearm and pointed it at Beck's skull. "Jew, do you think it is fair sport to chatter and spread misinformation?"

"I'm actually not a Jew, sir. I'm a pacifist, convicted of treason."

With that, Gessert paused, breathed in, and calmly adjusted the grip on his gun. He violently struck the gun against Beck's face. Beck crumpled to his knees.

"Insolent Jew!"

Beck rocked back and forth, holding his head in pain. "My apologies, sir. It's just that the colonel indicated that there was such an order. We've been besieged by so much Allied bombing lately. I mistakenly assumed that the colonel, corporal, and sergeant had received and followed the order."

Gessert held his pistol against Beck's skull. "Miserable Jew, prepare to die. Magnus, confirm for me that those two officers and the colonel are present in camp today."

An unearthly pause overtook the room.

"Begging your pardon, Captain, but the corporal and sergeant, appear to be absent today."

Gessert removed the end of the gun from Beck's skull. "What? Absent? Where are they?"

"Unknown, sir."

"Unknown? Deserters?"

Beck spoke again. "I presumed that they joined the colonel, Captain. Because of what the colonel had indicated about the order."

Gessert tapped his pistol gently against Beck's skull. "You have conversations with our colonel, about these matters, Jew?" The colonel is your dear friend?"

"No sir. The colonel never spoke to me directly about the order. But logic dictates that such an order exists. Either the lieutenant is lying about the colonel's presence in camp, which for a loyal SS officer is impossible, or such an order exists, and Lieutenant Magnus has simply not been informed of the order."

Gessert smiled and shook his head. He placed his pistol against Beck's forehead. "Jew, I would very much enjoy placing a bullet in your skull today, but I am in a great hurry. And I don't wish to trouble myself with the fuss of reloading my pistol."

Beck nodded.

"Private, no food or drink today for these Jews. They have a loudmouth in their midst who has decided this consequence for them."

"Yes, Captain!"

The three tersely left the barracks.

...

"Private, pour that food and water onto the field. Then continue with your assigned duties."

"Yes sir."

As Gessert and Magnus walked back, Gessert barked, "Indisposed or not, I will see the colonel, now!"

Inside, Magnus rapped gently on the colonel's office door. "Colonel Rettmund, Captain Gessert requires your presence." He rapped some more. "Colonel?"

"Get the key and open the door, Magnus."

"Yes sir." Magnus began to sweat profusely. He fumbled with the key and eventually unlocked and opened the door. Empty.

"So, where is the 'indisposed Colonel,' Magnus?"

"I don't know, sir. He had mentioned his concern about having sufficient fuel available for our camp. He may have driven into town to barter for some."

"He does that often? Barters with the villagers? Doesn't send a subordinate?"

"Ahh … yes, he does visit the village from time to time to replenish supplies."

"Is his staff car here?"

Magnus pulled the window shades apart. "It is not, sir."

"Very well. Make sure your report to the colonel includes the damage assessment as well as details on the two deserters. Gestapo will need to be informed. Oh. And kill the loudmouthed Jew. I believe there is a functioning crematorium here for disposal of the remains."

"Yes sir!"

"I will be back here tomorrow afternoon to see the colonel in person and receive the report."

"Yes sir!"

…

"Nice work, Beck. Today, we all starve."

Elias Matzner pointed to Beck. "Let him be, Levinsky. He's the one taking the beatings."

Beck waved Matzner off. "No, Lev is right, Elias. I'm sorry to cost everyone their food. But, that's two more Nazis we helped escape, Emmerich and Wittmer. Now there are just two more left."

Levinsky scowled. "Two Nazi pig deserters. I hope they both get their throats slit by the Resistance!"

Beck chuckled, "And even if they don't, they'll still get what they deserve."

"How so?"

"Remember when I told you about how an escapee carries his prison with him? The same applies to men consumed by evil. They shoulder the weight of their hatred constantly. The weight is enormous and eventually eats them alive. The good man, on the other hand, knows that kindness and mercy are never a burden. They lift the good man up. They actually lighten his load."

"More nonsense, Beck. Your words don't put food in my stomach."

…

Lieutenant Magnus sat in his office chair, dazed and sweating. The loudmouthed Jew prisoner had gotten him into a lot of trouble. He looked forward to firing a bullet into the back of his miserable skull. He thought about the colonel. Had he deserted? He said that he would only require two, maybe three days. He'd been gone a full week. *And if he's not back here by tomorrow afternoon when the captain returns, my career is over. Probably my life.*

He thought some more and realized it was already too late. His career was over. The two SS officers assigned to the camp had simply deserted … on his watch. And he had no explanation or information on how or why that could have happened. He thought back to the colonel. How, during dinners together, they had reminisced about earlier times when there was peace. When they were younger men with their lives and military careers ahead of them. The beautiful towns in which they grew up and prospered. Their families. He hated to consider it, but on reflection, the colonel must have simply deserted. And he would too.

He pulled a piece of stationery from his desk drawer and typed a short note.

"Colonel Rettmund, should you return, I have departed. This camp is no longer safe for me, nor for you. Lieutenant Magnus."

He folded the note in two and placed it on the colonel's desk. He stood over his own desk and placed his tiny wire-framed reading glasses and military ID on his desk blotter. He walked over to his room in the officers' quarters and changed out of his uniform, carefully hanging it in the wardrobe. He dressed in his civilian clothes and looked at himself in the mirror. He told himself that he was not deserting, because the war was as good as over. And with the war concluded, he was merely going back home to the beautiful town where his wife and family awaited. Dresden. There, he would be forever free of bombings.

As he seated himself in his staff car, he realized that he had forgotten to kill the Jew who had caused all of the trouble. But, wearing a freshly ironed shirt and clean necktie, he decided it wasn't worth the bother. *No point in getting bloodstains on my good clothes.* He opened the gate for himself and drove through the entrance, on to Dresden and freedom.

...

Bauer visited the bomb site. Two of three factory buildings were fully destroyed. Twisted shards of metal, once constituting machines, bulged through the remains of the roofs and walls. He walked, gingerly, along one of the nearby bomb craters. He lingered at the site because he had absolutely nothing else to do ... except to wait for the evening's Allied bombing runs.

As he wandered back toward his quarters, he spotted Magnus's staff car exiting the camp. He chuckled to himself. *The colonel and I are now the only German military remaining.* He decided to seek out the colonel for any further assignments. He entered the anteroom of the colonel's office and saw Magnus's ID and glasses on Magnus's desk. The colonel's door was partly ajar. Bauer tentatively entered the office. *Empty.* Bauer hadn't believed in all of Beck's talk about an evacuation order, but now he wasn't so sure.

He wandered over to the mess hall, hoping that one of the Polish women would come to feed him. They did not. He stopped into the kitchen and saw the women preparing the evening's gruel for the prisoners. As he suspected, the cooks used the same oatmeal he had been eating, just watered down in massive iron pots. He tried to speak to them, to tell them that the prisoners were not to be fed that evening. But they did not understand German. He pointed to a bowl of small French loaves and then to his own stomach. One of them nodded and handed him two loaves and an apple. He stood and ate before them. He didn't want to be alone. He was happy to be in a place where people seemed to know what was going on and had chores to perform. When he was done eating, he walked back to his quarters, laid down on his cot, and quietly wept.

. . .

The afternoon passed wearily. The prisoners were not talkative. Morale was low due to lack of food and water and the knowledge that their situation would only get worse as the hours passed. As dusk settled in, they heard the familiar sounds of the metal barrels being dragged toward the barracks. Several of the men stood and moved closer to the barracks door in anticipation.

Bauer unlocked the door and dragged the food and water barrels inside. "Yes, I'm not supposed to feed you."

Beck jumped up immediately to assist. "Thank you, Bauer. We appreciate your kindness!" Other prisoners repeated their own thanks, loudly.

"No kindness, Beck. The food was already made, and it should not go to waste."

"Of course! Are they still feeding you? Would you like to share in this?"

"I am fed."

"I ask because I know—we all know—what it's like to be alone. With Magnus having departed, and obviously with there being no actual colonel around."

"Why do you think Magnus is gone?"

"Stands to reason. He clearly lied about the evacuation order and knows he'll be found out. And of course, if the rumor about the French woman is true, he could be shot as a traitor. That's why he left.

"I'm sure Magnus's absence will all be rectified, soon enough. It doesn't concern me. And it should definitely be of no concern to you."

"Of course. And we are all still worried about your safety. Will you consider bunking with us this evening?"

"No, Beck. But thank you."

"May I ask you for one charity?"

"What?"

"Because of the risk you face in staying in your barracks in light of the bombings, would you consider leaving the barracks door unlocked for this evening? That way should something … happen to you, we would at least have a chance to survive. Otherwise, if something unfortunate were to happen, we would be trapped inside here without food and water potentially until we each died in here from starvation. Leaving the door unlocked would be the humane thing to do. And I, and each of us promise, that as long as we and you are alive, we will not try to escape from here."

With that, Bauer dragged the empty barrels out of the barracks and locked the door behind him.

…

"Nice try, Beck."

"Yes, but on a positive note, another down and only one more to go."

"Be quiet, Beck. We're all still angry at you for jeopardizing our lives … and your own." Levinsky snarled. "Yes, we care about your life, Beck. What would we do here without you? We'd miss the entertainment. None of us would agree to be slapped around like you."

"Thanks, Lev. The beatings are simply the cost of orchestrating the escape plan for the German soldiers. Bauer is last. But I've made a small adjustment to the plan. Bauer will not escape like the others. He, like the rest of us, will leave here as a free man. And he'll be back this evening to bunk with us."

"Why do you think that?"

"Because Bauer has a good heart. And wisdom. He knows he belongs with us. And I think you'll be pleased to hear some additional news. It's now time for me to reveal the plan. And I think you'll find it's simply an implementation of the plan that's been in effect all along … with a few minor variations."

…

Bauer stepped back into the kitchen just as the two Polish women were finishing the day's cleanup. He took four more small loaves with him from the bowl, which had been covered over with a tea towel. The women ignored him. He wandered back to his barracks, sat, and waited for the sounds of Allied aircraft.

…

Levinsky paced around the barracks in frustration. "Unlikely, Beck! Most unlikely! Your plan is completely ridiculous! How are you supposed to be released from here to get to the colonel's office? How can you accomplish all that you say you can accomplish in such a short period of time? Bauer is not going to unlock this prison for you. Everything you've outlined is complete and utter nonsense!"

"But you see how it makes sense. You feel in your soul that the plan *could* work."

Issac Cohen spoke up. "I think it could work. And even if it doesn't, I want to try it! I don't want to be here forever, starved or bombed to death!"

The prisoners unanimously voiced their agreement.

Levinsky scowled.

"Lev, we need you. Quite badly. And we need the boy, Bauer, too. Will you join us? Much will be asked of you. You may have to sacrifice even more than the others. But I know you will meet every challenge."

Levinsky sat on the straw-covered floor with his back against the cold woodstove. He clenched his fists and sighed loudly. "Yes.

Yes, Beck. I will go along with your ridiculous plan."

…

Bauer sat waiting on his cot. He mulled it over. The close proximity of the prior evening's bombings made the decision easier. He would bunk with the prisoners. He heard the first overhead, distant rumble, grabbed the loaves and his rifle, and made his way to B barracks.

The men heard the telltale sound of the door being unlocked and stood immediately. "I will stay with you tonight for my own safety. Here."

Bauer broke each of the loaves in two and passed them out to the others to share.

Eli Goldenberg bit into his piece. "Thank you, Bauer!" The rest of the men, with full mouths, mumbled their own thanks.

Beck spoke. "Bauer, we don't even know your first name?"

"It's Emil. Emil James Bauer."

"I would guess that you are about twenty or twenty-one years old."

"Twenty, Beck."

"That's a good age. When is your birthday?"

"Why does that matter?"

"Everyone has a birthday. A very special day. A day spent happily. Something to recollect."

"August 5th, 1924."

…

The night wore on, and the bombings began anew. The sounds of Allied aircraft pierced the sky, causing nausea and fear among the men. Thunderous, tremor-producing explosions followed. Many of the men placed their fingers in their ears against the deafening sounds. Several cried out. Bauer figured that the bombs must have struck the area of the camp closest to the factory buildings.

Beck yelled over the sounds. "Bauer, I have a confession to make. I don't know whether these barracks are all that safe. I had only supposed that the Allies knew this was a prison barracks. I didn't know such."

Bauer yelled back, "Fine, Beck. Bombs go where they please."

…

The bombing finally ended. No one slept, but they all survived. As day broke, Beck stood.

"Bauer, this is an important day for all of us. You know in your heart that unless we act, this will be the last day we all spend on earth."

Bauer hated to admit it, but he agreed. "And what of it, Beck? What can we do to stop the Allied attacks?"

"Very simple. We can all evacuate together. We can all leave this camp as free men. We, no longer as prisoners, and you, no longer in active military service. In a very short time, I will have access to identification papers and documents that will confirm that each of us former prisoners are, hereafter, free German citizens, no longer subject to seizure or arrest. Your identification papers will indicate an honorable discharge from the army for faithful service. You will then be free to return to your family."

Bauer shook his head. "And how is this miracle to occur?"

"As I told my colleagues, in the past I was a document examiner serving both private companies as well as our government. I was, and am, also a bit more than that. I am an authorized document signer for Heinrich Himmler and other generals and officials of the Reich. Although unknown to the public, orders, decrees, and other official documents requiring signatures are seldom signed by the given official. They are turned over to a few, specially trained signers such as myself, who sign the documents in the same hand as the official."

"Are you suggesting you can forge documents?"

"No. When I sign a document it is, by law, not a forgery. By law, my signature on a document has all the force and effect as the hand of the stated official. By law, such cannot be challenged, in any way, in any court or military setting. You can see how important this law is. If countless documents from Himmler or other officials could be impeached, the Third Reich and the war effort would crumble to dust under doubt and uncertainty. Thus, by statute, my hand is the same as the official's, even if the particular official did not specifically authorize the document."

"How can that be, Beck? Your signing authority must have been revoked when you were convicted."

"Ah, one would think. But it was not, for an important reason. Formal revocation requires an amendment to the statute. The statutes, of course, are published in the legal codes and law books, all public matters. If it became known that my authority was revoked due to my conviction, any or all of those past documents would then be impeachable. Important laws and decrees of the Third Reich could be questioned or ignored. But as long as the original statute serves without amendment, my signature is fully effective. No amendment has ever been enacted, so my authority remains intact. Remember that, to the Reich, the risk of a convicted person creating and signing new orders and documents is negligible. After all, such a convict is within secure prison walls or perhaps dead following execution. Do you see? *'L'État, c'est moi.'* And I am ready to grant us all our freedom."

Bauer gazed down on the ground in thought. He didn't want to die. He knew that even if he stayed, he could somehow still face blame for the desertions of the others, for not timely discovering and reporting their treason. For somehow facilitating their desertions. Not being SS and being a mere army private meant he would be an easy scapegoat. He had seen it before.

"Just how would you be able to sign such documents, Beck? You won't have any signature exemplars to copy from. You won't know how to create such documents."

"I have memorized all of the necessary signatures. I know exactly how the documents must read. I examined many such documents in the past. Thousands. And it's been said that I have a photographic memory. The only thing we need is a typewriter, pen, and paper. Presumably, the colonel's office has those."

"Yes, but every second you remain in the colonel's office at his typewriter increases the chance of being caught. The colonel could return at any time. You would need all day to type twenty-three original documents."

"No. Just one hour. And then we would leave."

"Where exactly would we be going?"

"To the Swiss border, where we'll cross into Switzerland as free men. If we encounter Nazis at the border, we will have our cover story and documentation. We will also have documents required by the Swiss to allow each of us to legally enter Switzerland."

Bauer shook his head in disbelief. "Switzerland is eighty miles away, Beck. Are we going to walk eighty miles, because there are no autos or trucks in this camp."

"Yes. We will travel through the forest adjacent to the road unless we chance upon some vehicle to commandeer. Even without a vehicle, we could be to the border in five days."

"You prisoners have no good shoes. Some of these men are wearing wooden shoes."

"We will share the best shoes we have among us. We will help each other."

"What will we eat?"

"We'll forage. We'll steal. There are many farms along the way. Many of the fields still have grain. The important point is that we have the will to do this. To not do this, for us at least, means death by bombings. Or, if we survive the bombings, execution, because once the Allies get close to the camp, we will not be worth evacuating. Exterminating us will be easier. So, as you see, this is our best and I believe only chance to survive."

Bauer looked to the faces of the prisoners. "I don't mind sleeping in the forest. I've roughed it before. But can you, men?"

The prisoners nodded their heads in assent. Most responded, "We will."

"Beck, if we are challenged along the way, what do we tell them that we are doing? It will look like a bunch of prisoners wandering in the forest."

"I and another of the men will be wearing German uniforms and will hold appropriate documents explaining our mission, our cover story. You will wear civilian clothes as a worker under my charge."

"Why wouldn't I just wear this uniform?"

"Because French Resistance fighters are likely in the forest. Even though none of us, including you, will have a weapon, a sniper may only see the uniform and shoot. That's why we two prisoners will wear the uniforms. To keep you out of danger."

"Why no weapons, Beck? I have my rifle."

"Yes, but neither you nor these men want to take a German life. We are still Germans, whether our country wants us or not."

"Are you sure, Beck? I wouldn't fire on a countryman, but I thought your men would if necessary."

"We will not. I am a pacifist. The plan depends on our not taking lives. Peace is our sword. When I was a young document examiner and signer, I was apathetic. Apolitical. I took no real interest in the Nazi movement. But after reading and signing hundreds and hundreds of documents of death, I could no longer continue. I refused to sign documents. Refused military service. Spoke out against the Reich. I became a pacifist. That's why I was convicted."

"If we leave here, we'll be sought by the SS, papers or not."

"That's true. Time will be of the essence. But I believe we will have a few days' head start. There's no one left in this camp to report us. The mysterious colonel may never return. If, in a few days' time, our absence is discovered, they will likely presume that we have fled for France, through Alsace. They won't expect us to be walking to Switzerland through the woods. By the time they discover that we did not flee to France, we could be at the Swiss border."

"But we shouldn't head toward France?"

"No. We would almost certainly meet German forces defending the Rhine against the Allies. Switzerland is safest."

Bauer looked to the ground again. He wrung his hands unconsciously. He thought of his wife and family back home. Their baby would turn two soon. "Okay, Beck. Let's implement your plan."

"Thank you, Bauer. Lev, Issac, come with Bauer and me. Men, stay put here until one of us returns to take you to the dining hall."

Goldenberg chimed in. "Are you saying we may be fed today, in the dining hall?"

"Yes."

With that the barracks exploded into cheers.

. . .

"Bauer, did any of those SS officers shed their uniforms before they escaped?"

"I'm not sure. We can check their quarters. You know, there's a pretty small chance that any uniform would fit men as bony as you."

"I know, but I'll make it work."

"Here's Lieutenant Magnus's uniform."

Beck held it up. "Perfect."

"I don't see any others here."

"Did young Hammel leave his uniform behind?"

"Yes, it's in his footlocker in our barracks."

The four walked briskly to the barracks building. They were surprised to see that part of the building had caved in, thanks to the prior evening's bombing.

Bauer pointed. "That's about where my cot had been."

They entered the barracks gingerly, hoping to avoid a further avalanche. Bauer opened the footlocker. They saw the uniform that had looked so comically large on Hammel.

"Hold it up, Lev, to see if it could fit."

"Me? Absolutely not!"

"What do you mean?"

"Beck, I am a Jew, and I refuse to wear the Nazi uniform. The uniform is an insult to my faith and my people."

"Lev, it's just pieces of cloth."

"Sure, you goyim don't understand or care anything about our laws. I will not bow down and worship pagan Nazi idols. I would rather be lowered into a blazing furnace to be burned alive!"

Beck looked at the three faces. "I think we are already in that furnace, Lev. I'm just here to hold back the flames."

Issac chimed in. "Beck, I agree with Lev. That is not something we Jews should do."

Bauer shrugged nonchalantly. "I'll wear mine. I'll take the risk about snipers. Like you said, Beck. I'll leave my rifle behind."

"Thanks, Bauer."

"I'll take the rifle, then, Bauer, if you won't."

"Lev, we all agreed. We won't carry such weapons. The rifle has to stay behind. It's part of the plan."

"Ridiculous, Beck. We'll need it to survive. To fight back."

"Lev, the rifle to me is like the uniform to you. But here—I have a compromise."

Beck reached into the footlocker and returned with the homemade, stubby club used by Hammel. "This is your weapon."

Levinsky scowled and looked over the amateurishly carved club. "Okay, Beck. You win. I'll take the club. And I'll take these boots, too." Levinsky picked up Hammel's pair of boots next to the footlocker and carefully sat down among the rubble. "Not a bad fit." He placed the club into the back of his right boot.

"Good, Lev. Bauer, does the colonel's office have a map of this region?"

"Yes. A large wall map. Probably others."

"Good. You and Lev go and bring the men to the dining hall. Issac and I will examine the route to Switzerland."

. . .

Beck opened Magnus's desk drawer and handed over a magnifying glass to Cohen. "Here, Issac." Cohen began running the magnifier along the wall map, identifying possible routes and making notes on a piece of camp stationery.

Beck changed into the uniform and adjusted it where he could. He found the tiny wire-rimmed reading glasses and put them on. He looked at Magnus's military ID. Beck held the ID open. "Issac, close enough?"

Cohen raised the magnifying glass first to the ID then to Beck's face. "With those little glasses, it could work."

"Good. I'll walk with you to the dining hall and then arrange the meal with the cooks in the kitchen."

...

The two Polish women in the kitchen chatted while preparing the day's gruel. They were surprised to hear a man behind them, speaking in Polish. They turned around to see a Nazi officer, one they had not seen before.

"Good morning, ladies! My name is Lieutenant Beck. I hope you'll be able to serve twenty-three men with officers' breakfasts. Now, I know you may not have prepared for this, but please use up all of the remaining food in your pantry and ice box for this breakfast, except for any foods you would like to take home to your own families. Today, your compulsory service in this camp ends. The gifts of food you take with you are in gratitude for your service."

The two women smiled broadly, thanked Beck profusely, and got to work.

...

Beck trotted back to Magnus's office. He found plain bond paper and began typing. He had memorized each man's full name, age, and date of birth. Much of the typing was rote repetition. Once he had completed typing all of the documents, he found Magnus's fountain pen and began carefully signing each. All in all, the entire process took less than one hour.

He folded up the completed documents into individual packets and dropped them into a large envelope. He entered the colonel's office and took a final look at the large map and the route that Issac had suggested. He glanced down at the colonel's desk and noticed the folded paper. He read the note and then tore it into tiny pieces for the rubbish can. As he was doing so, a Nazi staff car, followed by a nondescript black Gestapo sedan, entered the prison. The cars passed by the building and parked in the empty motor pool lot.

The men sat breakfasting boisterously in the dining hall. Although the portions were modest, the plates of cheeses, boiled eggs, smoked fish, jams, honey, apples, and steamed carrot slices were, to a man, the best food they had eaten in years. Beck had not joined them, but the men hadn't noticed.

Suddenly the jovial atmosphere in the dining hall was shattered by the piercing sound of a gruff German voice.

"What goes on here?" Why are these Jew prisoners in this dining hall?"

Every heart stopped. The men looked up to see a frightening Nazi major and young civilian man dressed in a long black leather coat. Nazis they had never seen before. Bauer's intestines churned. *Where the hell is Beck?*

The major pointed to Bauer. "You, Private. Explain yourself! Explain this!"

Bauer looked up to see yet another frightening Nazi officer enter the dining hall.

"Heil Hitler, Major. I am Lieutenant Otto Beck. These men are under my command."

Seeing Beck in full SS regalia caused the jaws of every prisoner to drop. Bauer thought, *Thank God!*

"I am Major Lindauer, and this is Agent Wolfe of the Gestapo. Where is your colonel? Explain why these prisoners are dining here!"

"I, too, sought out the colonel, as I am not permanently stationed at this camp. Regrettably, the colonel's whereabouts are unknown to me. I presumed that he received an evacuation order, as only these staff people are present in the camp. All prisoners, too, have apparently been evacuated."

"All prisoners? Who then are these Jews in prison uniforms?"

"These men are not prisoners, Major. They are former prisoners proven loyal to the Reich who have been recruited for a special project. They are agents with full German citizenship, irrespective of their Jewish blood."

"What special project? These men look too old and weak to hold a pickaxe, let alone undertake anything special! And by who's order were these Jews made German citizens?"

"Major, despite appearances, these men are quite capable. And the order granting citizenship is signed by Heinrich Himmler."

"Heinrich Himmler? Show me such orders, and produce your ID!"

Beck casually produced his recently manufactured ID, which used the photo taken from Magnus's own. He handed the ID over and squinted his eyes, trying to resemble Magnus's appearance in the photo as closely as possible.

Lindauer scrutinized the ID. The photo was not a great likeness, but the small glasses were the same. The document looked sufficient. He handed it over tersely to Wolfe who glanced it over and handed it back to Beck.

"And now the order about your mission and these prisoners."

"Yes, Major." Beck handed over a two-page, folded document with a bronze fastener in the corner. He sincerely hoped that the ink had dried. The major perused it carefully several times. He looked from the document to Beck and then to the frightened faces of the prisoners. He was in the process of handing the document over to Wolfe, when he felt his wrist being tapped, gently.

"I'm sorry, Major. I will have to see Agent Wolfe's papers, first. This order is of a highly secret nature. I shared it with you, sir, because of your superior rank. But I am not authorized to share it with others until I can confirm their credentials."

The flustered Major snarled at Wolfe. "Yes, show him your papers."

Angrily, Wolfe produced his Gestapo photo ID. "Here, Lieutenant!"

Beck perused the document carefully. "Sufficient, Agent Wolfe. Sufficient. Here is the order."

Wolfe greedily pawed the order, going over it line by line, carefully scrutinizing Heinrich Himmler's signature. He handed the order back over to Beck, icily.

Lindauer was still not comfortable. The men looked too diseased, too beaten down, too old. Jews they certainly were, but citizens of the Fatherland, with full rights and privileges? "The order states that these men are involved in espionage on behalf of the Reich."

"That's correct, Major. Some will be positioned within other camps as spies to root out Resistance sympathizers. Others will assist in acts of intelligence-gathering and sabotage."

"You say they have special skills and training. Perhaps a test is in order?"

"Certainly, Major. I will call out the name of an agent and they will provide their name and specialty for you. Hirsch Wenig."

Wenig immediately stood sharply at attention and provided a proper military salute. "Heil Hitler, Major Lindauer. Hirsch Wenig, procurement."

"Procurement, Wenig? Tell me how you accomplish this with so many shortages?"

"Barter and bribery for the most part, sir. Usually involving multiple parties."

"Of course. Something where your Jew blood comes in handy."

Wenig remained stiffly at attention and did not react to the slight.

"Be seated. Let me pick one, Beck."

"Certainly, sir."

Beck was hoping that the others, knowing of Wenig's military background, would imitate Wenig's demeanor when called upon.

"You there. Stand." Lindauer pointed to Goldenberg.

"Heil Hitler, Major! Eli Goldenberg. Watchmaker." Goldenberg awkwardly saluted, trying to mimic Wenig to the best of his abilities.

"Watchmaker? And that has some special value to the Reich?"

Beck spoke. "Yes, Major. For timing devices for bombs. For sabotage against the Resistance."

"Be seated. You. Stand."

"Heil Hitler, Major. Issac Cohen, cartographer." Cohen's salute and stance were a bit sharper than Goldenberg's.

"Ah, cartography. How fortunate. That is one of my hobbies. Tell me, Cohen, the latitude and longitude for Berlin."

Cohen looked down to the ground and then back up to the ceiling. "Latitude 52.5° North, longitude 13.4° East. These are approximations, sir."

"Impressive, Cohen. How about … New Delhi?"

"Hmm. New Delhi. Latitude 28.6° North, longitude 77.2° East. Again, approximations, sir."

Lindauer grumbled to himself. He looked over to the right side of the hall and saw one man trying to avert his eyes, looking downward, scowling.

"You there. You look familiar to me. Do I know you?"

A wave of fear passed through Levinsky. He stood. But he would not salute the Nazi. He could not. But then he did. "Heil … sir. Evan Fromme …. Ah … symphony composer."

"Symphony composer? Well, there's something I know nothing of. Music is a wasteful pastime which robs the spirit and the intellect. I don't care for music." He looked more closely at Levinsky. "Have we met, Fromme?"

Levinsky tried to avoid his usual scowl. He smiled, producing an audacious rictus grin. "No, Major, sir. We have not." He grinned some more.

Beck interjected. "Mr. Fromme is more than a symphony composer, Major. Fromme encodes important information and communications into his symphony scores. The Allies have never broken his codes. This is top secret within the Reich. And explains Mr. Fromme's seeming eccentricity."

"Of course. Of course."

"Would you honor us with your presence for breakfast, Major and Agent Wolfe? The food is quite serviceable."

Lindauer looked over to his nephew. "Yes, why not."

Slowly, the conversations grew louder and men more relaxed.

"Beck, I am impressed that your special Jews are willing to continue to travel in their filthy prison uniforms. They are either stupid or as dedicated to the Führer as we are."

"They are quite dedicated, sir. They understand that to gain information, they must blend in with the prison populations where they are assigned. Those not assigned to prisons must present themselves as prison escapees, willing to take on dangerous work. Only by blending into their surroundings and playing their roles will they receive the valuable intelligence we require. Intelligence that will crush the French Resistance. They are not afraid to look and act the part of the common Jew prisoner for the good of the Reich. Exceptional men."

The Polish women brought out several large fruit pies. Everyone enjoyed their fill. The conversation slowly subsided.

"We have other camps to inspect, Beck. Wolfe and I wish you great success."

"Why thank you, Major and Agent Wolfe, I feel certain we shall succeed."

…

Finally, they were gone.

"Lev, did you know those men?"

Levinsky scowled. "Yes, Beck. Lindauer was the officer who sent me to the camps … because I scowled."

The men laughed.

"Well, nice improvisation, Mr. Bach. And speaking of which, because of this unexpected contact with Lindauer and the Gestapo, the plan will require a few minor refinements."

Levinsky sighed. "What do you mean, Beck?"

"I had hoped that we would have several days' head start and wouldn't need to use our cover story until we reached the border. That is no longer the case. It won't take them long to realize that we had no trucks or autos parked in the car park. They'll wonder how we got to Natzweiler-Struthof without transportation. They'll wonder why we happened to be there in the first place. They'll try to confirm our cover story."

Goldenberg interjected. "So, what are you saying, Beck? Do we continue?"

"We do, Eli. But I fear that by the time we reach the Swiss border, the SS and Gestapo will be patrolling heavily, looking for a fake SS officer and a band of men in prison garb. Although our papers will be fine once we cross the border, we won't be able to use our papers at the formal crossing. We will have to cross surreptitiously, over a wall or fence, just as smugglers do. In other words, the risk for each of us is greater now."

Beck paused and looked out among the disappointed faces.

"It's still not too late for any man to drop out. Bauer, you in particular should consider doing so. You could claim that you were overpowered by the prisoners at a feeding. That we forced you at gunpoint to accompany us at the dining hall. That you could not speak out at the time, because you were still held at gunpoint. Those choosing to stay could go back to prison. You could claim that you were able to recapture those. That should be enough to keep you safe, Bauer. If you do choose to stay, we would only ask that you give us a three-hour head start before contacting your superiors."

Bauer looked down to the ground and wrung his hands together. He looked back up to Beck. "I choose to leave with the rest of you. We will find a way over the border."

"Thank you, Bauer! Does anyone else intend to stay behind?"

No man spoke.

"Good. It's time for us to begin our journey."

…

"Beck, once we leave camp, our best route is first straight ahead into the forest, due east. The topographic map indicated that we will eventually come upon a fairly large creek. Almost certainly, a trail will run alongside the creek. We would then follow the trail for as long as possible due south, toward Switzerland."

"Then that's what we'll do, Issac. Bauer, you and Issac lead the way. I'll take up the rear. Where possible, we'll walk double file."

The first day's travel through the forest had been more pleasant than expected. The weather was mild, and the fall foliage had turned to tones of yellow, orange, and bronze. Although they found no foods to forage, they came upon the creek as predicted by Cohen, which provided fresh water. The group had to take several rest breaks throughout the day due to the age and frailty of several of the men, but they made excellent progress in their journey. As night fell, they huddled together in a clearing. They heard the rumble of Allied bombers and explosions. But, unlike past nights, they now knew they were safe from immediate harm. The men took turns sleeping under a now full moon.

...

"Major Lindauer, I apologize for calling you at this time of the evening. I hope I am not interrupting your dinner."

He was. Lindauer scowled while chewing on his piece of chicken cordon bleu. "What is it, Gessert?"

"I returned to Natzweiler-Struthof to meet with the colonel to collect the damage assessment from the recent Allied bombings as well as a full report on the apparent desertion of two officers. I also required Magnus to provide me with an audience with the colonel, as the colonel had declined to see me the day before and then absented himself later, I believe, to avoid me."

"Desertions?"

"Yes, Major. A very irregular situation. Apparently two officers assigned to Magnus deserted the evening before I arrived. Of course, I performed my duties and inspected the prisoners and their barracks, which were satisfactory. And I told Magnus that I would be back in person, today. When I arrived an hour ago, I discovered the entire camp deserted. The colonel, notwithstanding my demand, was not present, nor was Magnus. Even the staff were absent. More importantly, the prisoners were also missing. I thought that some sort of evacuation had occurred. However, I was never provided any advance notice about this evacuation. So, with all due respect, I am calling to find out whether such an evacuation order was issued."

Lindauer responded angrily. "I know of no evacuation order, Gessert! When Wolfe and I did our unscheduled review this morning, the colonel likewise was not present, at least according to Lieutenant Beck."

"Lieutenant Beck, sir?"

"Yes, one of Herr Himler's pet projects. Beck was running a team of ex-prisoners trained in espionage. I had never met Beck before, but his documents were in order."

"Did you happen to observe, sir, whether Magnus or other officers were present in the camp."

"I did not. Those matters concern you, Gessert, not me."

"Of course, sir. And presumably you didn't observe the prison barracks at that time?"

Lindauer sighed. "Of course not, Gessert. That is one of your responsibilities."

"Sir, you mentioned prisoners being used in Herr Himler's project. Did you see those prisoners?"

"Yes, I did. About twenty Jews in tattered uniforms. To be inserted into other camps as spies for the Reich."

Gessert gulped. "About twenty."

"Yes."

"You said a Lieutenant Beck ran the mission. Do you recall the lieutenant's given name?"

"Yes. Otto. Otto Beck."

Gessert felt nauseous. "I believe we may have been deceived, sir. The name Otto Beck was the name given by a particularly glib Jew who I had ordered executed by Magnus. And now Magnus has disappeared."

. . .

The following morning, Beck declared, "Today, we will look for food." Cohen reviewed his hand drawn map identifying possible farms, based on the maps he'd studied in the colonel's office. The group gamely made their way through thicker forest toward the farm areas.

Unseen by the group were the two riflemen positioned nearby. The older, more experienced of the two lined up a shot on the

SS officer. An SS officer brought the best bounty, a cash prize, dependent on rank. The younger man targeted the regular army private. They both were curious about the odd scene: prisoners being marched into the forest and not on the road. They were about to fire when the older man said, "Wait."

They watched as the SS officer caught up with a prisoner in the middle of the pack who had stumbled and was having difficulty walking. They watched the SS officer take the man by his waist to help him walk. The rifleman also noticed that the SS officer wore no sidearm. The older man said, "Hold your fire. We'll follow them."

By noon, the group had reached a working farm. Beck directed the men to stay behind in the woods. He took Bauer with him. They caught sight of a farmer pitching straw beside a barn.

"Sir, I am Lieutenant Beck, and this is Private Bauer. We're hoping you may have food that you would be willing to share with us. Anything in any amount would be appreciated."

The farmer ignored Beck and walked into his barn. Immediately, two men walked out of the barn, pointing rifles directly at Beck and Bauer, who instinctively raised their hands to the air.

"Who are you? Why are you out here in the woods with prisoners?"

Beck listened to the man's broken German, spoken with an Alsatian dialect. He responded in French. "We were prisoners, recently liberated from Natzweiler-Struthof, except for this man, who was not a prisoner, but is with us." He pointed to Bauer.

"Who liberated you? Allied troops have not advanced this far into the country."

Beck again pointed to Bauer. "This man, Emil Bauer, who had been serving as a private. He helped us."

"Why are you wearing the uniform of an SS officer?"

"As a disguise should we encounter any Nazi soldiers. We are traveling to the Swiss border where we will enter as free men."

The two riflemen looked from one to the other.

"You have a long journey ahead of you."

"Yes, we're hoping to find someone with a truck that would be willing to help us."

"We are a day away from a working truck. We travel here on foot. We hunt and kill Nazis for the bounty. And perhaps the sport. Do you have ID?"

"Yes, I created the document." Beck passed over his ID.

"It's a good forgery. It looks real. If I kill you, I will still earn the bounty, forged ID or not. And a good one, because you are lieutenant."

"Understood. But I am already dead. Whether back at the camp or here, now. You will have to make the choice."

"Do you have money?"

"Very little. Emil Bauer has a small amount left after giving most to a German boy volunteer so that the boy could go safely back home to his parents."

"Stay here." The two riflemen returned to the barn.

Bauer looked over to Beck. "What's going on?"

"These men are Resistance bounty hunters. They won't kill us, but they will want whatever money you have."

The two returned from the barn, with rifles at their sides. The older one spoke. "Hand over all the money you have."

Beck translated and Bauer emptied his pockets, handing over a few small bills and three coins.

"Yes. Very little money. Do you have any weapons?"

"No. We are pacifists and travel unarmed."

"Fools. You are no help to us. This man will feed you eggs.

That's all he has to offer. He's expected to deliver his meats and grains to the Nazis. He can spare little for you. How many are you?"

"Twenty-three."

"Bring your men into the barn."

After a few minutes, the farmer returned with two large pots of boiled eggs. He laid the two pots to the ground. "Hot. Let them cool."

The men formed a line much like they had inside their prison barracks. Each man scooped out a single egg by hand. The farmer pointed to a small well about fifty paces outside the barn. "There, for water."

The men, again, took turns drinking from the well bucket. The riflemen were surprised at how organized the prisoners were. How they didn't fight over the food and well water.

Beck spoke to the older one. "You mentioned that there's a truck about a day's distance from here. Were you heading back to the truck? Can we accompany you?"

"We are heading back. We will walk with you."

The farmer came out one more time and handed the older rifleman an ancient revolver. "Only three bullets."

Beck watched the farmer disappear inside his farmhouse. "I'd like to thank him for the food. Will he be back out?"

"He will not. Thank us for the food, Otto Beck. We arranged it. You see, he helps us only because we blackmail him. He is no friend. And here. This is for you. I promise, you will need it."

Beck received the gun, gratefully. "Thank you." He tucked the gun into his waistband and nodded in appreciation.

Levinsky was shocked. *Some pacifist.*

Beck spoke loudly enough for all the men to hear. "We will follow these two men today. There may be a truck we can use."

As they followed the riflemen, Levinsky walked next to Beck.

"Why did you accept the gun? Are you, now, willing to use the gun?"

"Lev, first, as you know, one should never turn down a gift. And, yes, I will use the gun." Beck removed the three bullets from the chambers and placed them in his uniform pocket. He jammed the unloaded gun into his waistband.

Levinsky shook his head and scowled. "You have to keep the bullets in the gun to be able to shoot it, Beck."

…

The day's journey through the woods was difficult. Several large brooks had to be crossed. Although the temperature was moderate, the knee-deep water was icy and chilled the men. Several steep hills had to be mounted, and Beck, Levinsky, and Bauer helped the physically weaker men along.

They could smell the farm before they saw it. A large dairy farm, their destination. The older rifleman assembled the group outside the farm against the setting sun.

"This is the farmer with the truck. He, like most of the farmers here, doesn't care about sides or loyalties. They care about money and surviving. I will bring him out."

After a few minutes, an old farmer with an austere gaze emerged from his farmhouse.

"These are the men looking for shelter and your truck. We leave you now." And with that the two riflemen disappeared into the setting sun.

Beck attempted to shake hands with the farmer. The farmer did not respond. Beck spoke in French, "Sir, my name is Otto Beck. We are men liberated from a concentration camp. We seek a ride in your truck to the Swiss border or as far in that direction as possible."

The man shook his head. "No. No truck without payment."

Beck removed the handgun from his waist and handed it over to the farmer. "We have no money. This is the only thing we have in trade." He rifled through his pocket and handed over the three bullets.

The farmer looked the revolver over carefully. "Not enough. I need more."

"Is there any work we could do here? Several of us are able-bodied."

The farmer looked off into the distance. "Can you load haybales into a truck? They are heavy."

"We can."

The farmer beckoned the men into his barn. "See?" He pointed to an enormous pile of haybales. "These must be loaded into the truck at daybreak. If you get them all in the truck, I will let you ride among the bales. I take these to a Nazi stable about thirty miles from the border. But I will first stop at the home of a woman with a car. She drives for money. Pay her and maybe she'll drive you to the border. Sleep here in the barn." As he walked away to the farmhouse he said, "No food tonight. Eggs in the morning once the hens have laid. Water is there." He pointed to a large stone wash tub.

The men listened to Beck's translation. Lev grumbled. Wenig spoke. "I can help load the haybales too, Beck. I'm strong enough." Others quickly volunteered.

"Thanks, men. Whoever is able can help."

As the men settled in to sleep, Beck said to Levinsky, "See. I told you I would use the gun."

...

Colonel August Rettmund had enjoyed his holiday away from the camp. The occasion of his daughter's wedding had been joyous. His son-in-law was a loyal member of the party, quickly rising in reputation. *Soon, he will be in the Führer's inner circle.* Rettmund didn't look forward to returning. The camp would be nearly empty, save for the planned arrival of a handful of useless Jew prisoners who couldn't be situated in the filled sub-camps. Rettmund knew he had overstayed his holiday. But, once he was home, there were so many friends and family members to socialize with. Pleasant meals and conversations just as in the old days. He felt a little bad for Magnus, who he'd left to run the camp on his own. He knew he should have returned much sooner. But to what end? What was there really for him and Magnus to do? He comforted himself with the thought. He came to the camp entrance and was surprised to find the gatehouse unattended. He unlatched the gate and drove his staff car to his motor pool lot adjacent to his office. He would send Magnus or one of the other subordinates down to relatch the gate later.

...

Herrman Schroeder made the turn into camp and was surprised to find that the gate had already been opened for him. *How could they know that I would make their delivery today?* He drove his truck to the dining hall building and waited. He knew that in a moment he'd see the two old Polish women come out to unload his truck. Technically, unloading was his job, but offering a piece of chocolate for the two old women to share always ensured that they would handle the work instead.

He noticed a staff car parked next to the colonel's office and hoped that the colonel was in. After the women unloaded, he would stop in to see the colonel, to apologize and explain that the delay in delivery was caused by the Allied bombings. So many unpassable roads. He would also inform the colonel that he was able to procure a case of the colonel's favorite Fronsac.

As Schroeder sat waiting for the Polish women to come out, he saw a black sedan pull into the camp. He watched the auto proceed rapidly to the building housing the colonel's office. He saw the occupants disembark, two likely Gestapo men in long, dark outer coats. Moments later, he watched in stunned silence as the Gestapo men, one on each side, virtually dragged the colonel out of his office in handcuffs. The colonel was writhing, twisting his neck from one man to the other, yelling, "Lies! Lies!"

Schroeder watched as the dark sedan left the camp at breakneck speed. He looked around. *And still no Polish women.*

…

Precisely at daybreak, Beck heard the rumbling sounds of a diesel engine approaching the barn. The truck was enormous. The farmer directed Beck on the placement of the bales in the truck. The most able-bodied of the men formed a bucket brigade to transfer the bales from the barn to the truck bed. Levinsky, Bauer, and Beck shouldered the worst of the burden. They left room among the haybales so that the men could squeeze in between stacks. Afterward, they watched as the farmer and a woman brought out two large skillets of scrambled eggs and two large ladles.

The men, as usual, lined up at the skillets, taking only one ladleful first before getting back in line. The woman said, "I will bring more," in broken German.

After eating, the farmer directed the men to the truck bed. He and Beck spread an enormous tarpaulin over the men and haybales in the bed. The farmer told Beck to sit up front with him in the cab. "No one will question my load if they see you."

…

The drive took about an hour. Despite being stuck under a bad-smelling tarp and breathing in diesel fumes, morale among the men was high. Finally, they felt the truck shift into low gear, turn, and slowly come to a stop. Beck and the farmer stripped back the tarpaulin. The men squinted and shielded their eyes in the blaze of the midday sun. They were surprised to find that they had driven up a driveway to a stylish, stone country home, featuring a large shed to the rear. Beck presumed the shed housed the auto.

A young woman, hearing the engine noise, came out of the home with a raised pistol. "Is that you, Bruckner? Why are you here? Why did you bring these men here?"

Beck interjected. "Ma'am, my name is Otto Beck. This is not my uniform. It's a disguise. We are men liberated from Natzweiler-Struthof. We are making our way to the Swiss border, to live free. We are unarmed."

"I am Claire. I don't appreciate men showing up unannounced at my doorstep. This is not an inn."

"My apologies. We came because we understand that you have an auto and sometimes transport people for a fee. Would you consider us as customers? If not, we will leave your home, immediately, and continue our walk to the border on foot."

The farmer interrupted. "Claire, I must get back on my route to the stables. They have no guns, and I believe them when they say they will walk."

"Yes, Bruckner. Go."

She looked over to Beck. "There are many men here. The border is an hour's ride. What do you offer in payment to get your men as close to the border as I safely can?"

Beck looked on solemnly. "We have no money. This man, Emil Bauer, who helped liberate us, gave nearly all of his money to a young boy who had been volunteering for the army. So that boy could get out of imminent danger and return to his parents."

"That's a wonderful story. But I transport for money, not stories."

"We could pay you back once we cross the border. We could send you money from Switzerland."

"Why would I trust you? A prisoner dressed up like a Nazi. It seems you are quite willing to deceive."

"That is true, Claire. I've spent the better part of a week lying to every Nazi I've encountered. I would not blame you for having suspicions. But may I ask one small kindness? May the men draw water from your well before we undertake the rest of our journey on foot?"

She pointed. "Yes, over there," and went back into her home.

Although disappointed, the men were glad to drink the well water, some of the purest they had encountered.

Within a few minutes, Claire returned, this time with another young woman.

"Beck, this is my sister, Olivia."

Olivia spoke. "What was the boy's name who was traveling back to his parents?"

"It was Hammel." Beck looked over to Bauer and asked in German, "What was Hammel's given name?"

"I don't actually know, Beck. I only knew him as Hammel."

Olivia responded. "I understood what he said. I found the boy in Rothau, near your camp. He looked lost, and I asked him in German if I could help. He asked me for a ride and paid me. I took him to his parents who were extraordinarily pleased. In learning of the small fee paid, they paid me much more, out of gratitude."

"That's good news! We had hoped for such a result for the boy."

"Do you recall some sort of club or stick that he carried?"

"Yes. Handmade."

"Where did you last see this club?"

"Well, right there." Beck pointed to Levinsky. "Lev, the boy's club. Do you have it?"

Levinsky, puzzled, produced the club from his boot and handed it to Beck.

"This is the club." He handed it to Claire.

"Good. Wait."

At that, the two women returned to the home. Within a few minutes they were back outside.

"We will exchange the transport for the club. When Olivia took the boy home, the boy thought he left it in the auto or maybe the town somewhere. He seemed very attached to that club. Olivia rechecked the auto and found nothing. We can tell his parents it was jammed under the backseat and was found. I believe they will pay us more out of gratitude."

"That is fortunate."

"Only a few men will fit in the auto, and we can't shuttle men back and forth to the border all day. There is a man with a truck who will come by tomorrow. He brings us things to … distribute. I will suggest that he take you. He and I will strike a deal. That is the best we can do. If you choose this, you and your men must stay out of sight today in the shed. Otherwise, please move on."

"We will stay, gladly. Thank you. We're also looking for someone to help us cross. Someone who may be willing to guide us to a breach in the fence."

Claire's facial expression turned solemn. "Well, that is a much more expensive and complicated matter. Have you heard of passeurs? These are men and women who smuggle Jews and others out of Germany. Their fees, like the risks they undertake, are high. I know several. But how would you possibly pay for all of these men?"

"I couldn't. I could commit to sending money once settled in Switzerland."

"That won't work. The passeurs know that there's no incentive to do so once you have crossed."

"I understand. Perhaps the best we can do is to be driven as close to the border as feasible. We can then continue in the woods and search for our own breach in the fence."

"The woods are filled with Nazis, smugglers, bounty hunters, and killers. Without the help of passeurs, you will never find a way over. You are merely dreaming."

"I understand. But sometimes dreaming is the best we can do … all we can do."

"True. My dream is to put each Nazi into a camp and have them suffer the way we have. My mother was a Jew, and my father a Catholic. They were executed by the Gestapo for 'making trouble.' For resisting the confiscation of their lands and property by the Nazis by taking the Reich to court. The proceedings became moot after their murders. My family lost their ancestral estate, farm, artwork, gold, everything. My sister and I were left with almost nothing. We survive thanks to the family car, which we were allowed to keep, provided we always gave priority to transporting Nazis at their whim. Otherwise, we spend our days transporting black market goods and people for a fee. Or hunting for gasoline."

"Which is why I appreciate your helping us even more."

"You're welcome. Someday we will get our revenge. We will cut the hands off of each of the Nazi thieves who stole our land."

"I understand. We all hate the evils perpetrated by the Nazis. Even I, as a pacifist, often harbor such feelings, as much as I try not to."

"A pacifist? What, do you 'love your enemies' and 'turn the other cheek'?"

Beck laughed. "I don't have any enemies. They may have me, but I don't have them. I never have to turn the other cheek because before I can, a Nazi has already slapped it!"

Claire barked out a solitary laugh. "You're a funny man, Beck!"

"Thank you! Loving an enemy seems a high hurdle. If you can't, it's probably better to ignore them than hate them. Feeling hate for an enemy never harms them. But it does harm you. Ignoring them takes far less effort."

"Probably good advice. Tell your men to settle inside the shed, out of sight. There are many eyes out there. The shed has a rear exit that leads to my well and beyond that, an outhouse. Be careful not to be seen. At sundown, I will bring you bread and maybe some fruit."

...

Beck explained his conversations with Claire to the men. "We'll hide in this shed today and stay overnight. Tomorrow, a man with a truck will arrive. Claire believes she can negotiate with him to take us as close to the border as possible. We'll go back to the woods and travel south until we reach the border."

Levinsky smirked. "You said we would be free men, Beck. Look at us. We may not have brought our prison with us, but nevertheless, here we are again behind four walls."

Beck smiled. "Yes, Lev, but this is a prison of our own choosing. And a temporary one, at that."

"Fine, Beck. So tomorrow we reach the border. How do we get over barbed wire?"

"Smugglers have routes through the border fences. We'll search for an existing breach. That's how we'll get to freedom."

Levinsky scowled. "And if we find no breach?"

"We'll make our own."

"With what tools?"

"We'll find tools."

"Unlikely, Beck. Most unlikely."

...

At dusk, Claire and Olivia entered the shed with sacks of bread loaves and pears. Claire began handing out bread from her sack "This is to be shared among everyone." Olivia handed each man a hard pear.

"Thank you, Claire and Olivia."

The other men joined Beck with their thanks.

"After this, try to sleep. You will need it for tomorrow."

…

In the morning, Claire handed out more bread loaves. "Be patient and remain inside here. The truck will be here soon enough."

Within an hour, Beck heard the sound of a truck rumbling up the driveway. Claire called the men out of the shed. Beck watched as Claire directed the driver to unload two small, unmarked kegs and two wooden boxes into the shed. Beck then watched as a man dressed in hunting gear emerged from the passenger side of the truck holding an opened, break-action shotgun. Beck watched the three converse. The truck driver shook his head in disagreement. The conversation grew louder and more contentious. Finally, the conversation quieted. Claire motioned for Beck to join them in the discussion.

"Beck, I was able to make some arrangements last evening. This man with the gun is a passeur. His name is Clef. I have paid for his services on behalf of you and all the men. I've done this not as a charity for you, but rather as a reprisal against the Nazis. The driver will take you to a place south of here called Hégenheim, near the border. From there, Clef will lead you into the forest to a place where you can pass through to Switzerland. The truck driver will continue through the border and meet Clef and your men at a place in Allschwil, just over the border. There, the driver will transport you to a building where men will help you with food and clothes. They will help your men blend into the background. From there, each will be on their own, as it would be too dangerous to move as a pack."

"Thank you, Claire! This is a tremendous gift. I hope to find some way to repay you someday."

"You won't be able to, Beck. And for both our sakes, I hope to never see you again."

Beck explained the plan to the men, who murmured their thanks to Claire. As Claire returned to her home, Beck withdrew the envelope he had maintained under his uniform shirt. He handed out a packet of papers to each man.

"Men, these are your papers. With these, you are free."

The men looked them over with curiosity. Wenig spoke. "These look quite authentic, Beck. Thank you." Others joined in the thanks.

"You're welcome."

The driver directed the men to lie down in the truck bed. He pointed to Beck. "You will sit next to me, up front."

The hunter handed his shotgun to Beck and helped the driver draw a large, dark tarpaulin over the truck bed. Beck handed the gun back to the hunter and sat in the front cab of the truck between the two men.

The truck, filled with its human cargo, rumbled down the driveway toward the main road. The driver turned the truck onto the road, but heading north.

"Clef, isn't the border behind us, in the other direction?"

He did not respond.

"Where are you taking us?"

After a lengthy pause, Clef responded. "We are taking you back to Natzweiler-Struthof."

"May I ask why?"

"Because you are worth money to us. They are searching for you. Didn't you know? Quite a lot of Nazis about, just itching to find you."

"If it's money you need, I can provide that. But you need to follow Claire's plan and take us to the border, as agreed."

"No. We have our own plan."

"May I offer an alternative plan?"

"No."

The truck continued northward for another ten minutes in silence.

...

"Bauer, they've headed in the wrong direction!"

"I know, Levinsky. I know."

"Why do you think they've done that? Maybe to pick up something they need?"

"Possibly. Or maybe to send us back to prison for a reward."

"Damn it!"

"Have hope, Levinsky. I have no doubt that Beck will talk them out of it."

...

After a gut-wrenching silence, Clef finally spoke. "How much money do you have, Beck?"

"No money with me, but endless funds once I get to freedom. More than you can imagine."

Silence, again, overtook the truck cab.

"Here's an idea, Beck. We will take these men back to Natzweiler-Struthof for the bounty, but bring you back with us. We will get you over the border. You will then direct the money we require from Switzerland to Claire. She won't know what it is for, but we'll collect it from her. This we will do for you. And then you will be free."

Beck looked down to his shoes for a few moments, as though contemplating the offer. "I have an even better idea. Because of my treachery in using an SS officer's uniform and facilitating our liberation from the camp, the bounty on my head, alone, will be quite large. Enormous, in fact. If you promise to get these men over the border, as planned, I will stay behind with you, and you may offer me to the highest bidder—SS, Gestapo, whomever. You will get more money that way and won't have to deal with twenty-two men who may make trouble for you. I promise I will be no trouble for you. I will go willingly."

"We could do that, Beck. They will execute you, of course."

"Yes, I know. In Germany I am already dead. So, it wouldn't matter."

The truck continued north to a clearing. The driver turned the truck around and headed back south toward the border.

...

The truck drove slowly and carefully. It pulled off onto a side road and bounced another ten minutes over a bumpy trail to a cemetery in the woods. The truck finally came to a stop. Clef directed Beck to assist with removing the tarpaulin. The men slowly righted themselves and disembarked, shakily, from the truck bed. Without a word, the truck driver drove away in the empty truck.

Clef addressed the men in broken German. "Follow me. Beck stays with me up front. Soldier, you take to the rear. Absolute silence. We move very slowly. If I crawl, you crawl. If I lie down, you lie down."

The men nodded in assent. They formed a line and followed Clef and Beck into the woods. The journey was slow and deliberate. At various points, Clef would motion everyone down to the ground while he listened.

After about twenty minutes of walking, Clef whispered to Beck, "This is a dangerous part. We are behind some farms close to a small village. But this is where we pass."

Slowly, Clef led the men along the rear line of a harvested field toward an enormous barbed wire fence. They stopped just at the edge of the field. "From here to the fence will be the most dangerous part. We will be in the sight of anyone on the village road. We will wait here just a little longer until twilight. Beck, move carefully along the line to the rear and tell the men that we wait here until dusk. Position yourself at the end with the soldier."

"Aren't you afraid I will run off?"

"No, Beck. Before was a test to see if you could be trusted. You will stay in line to cross the border too."

Beck quietly let the men know the plan and moved to the rear with Bauer and Levinsky.

"Beck, why did the truck head away and then turn back around?"

"Long story, Lev. We are at the dangerous part now, where we will be exposed. That's why we wait a little longer."

…

Within ten minutes, Clef signaled to the men to follow. He began crawling toward the barbed wire fence, the men likewise crawling behind. Beck watched as Clef reached the fence and with gloved hand began twisting at sections near the ground with pliers, exposing a precut flap of fence large enough for a man to crawl through.

Clef crawled through the opening on his belly. Once through, he held back the barbed flap and secured it out of the way with two large hooks. He whispered to the first man in line, "Do the same as me. On your belly and crawl through."

Beck watched as the men slowly crawled forward, to be pulled through the opening by Clef. He saw the truck driver in the distance at the edge of the woods motioning for each man to stay low and crawl toward him.

After about half the men had made it through, Beck heard sounds he so desperately did not want to hear: an auto screeching to a halt followed by the grinding gears of a truck braking. And then, loud German voices and barking dogs.

"There, Major! See, there! Get the dogs! Halt! Halt!"

Clef whispered loudly, "Hurry! You must hurry!"

Amid the sound of rifle fire, the line of men crawled faster and faster through the opening, with Clef frantically pulling each man through like rag dolls. "Hurry! Hurry!" Beck looked behind and realized that not all the men would make it through in time. He stood and yelled.

"Hold your fire! I am Lieutenant Otto Beck! Cease your fire at once!" The gunfire ceased, while more men were pulled through.

Suddenly an angry German voice screamed, "Imposter! Imposter! Shoot that man! Shoot to kill!"

Bauer tapped the shoulder of the last man, Levinsky. "Go, Levinsky! Go through!"

Gunfire pierced the air. Beck waved his arms before him. "Catch me! Catch me!" Beck then ran away from the line toward the village road.

More gunfire rang out in their direction. Bauer felt a stinging sensation in his hip and dropped to the ground, just outside the fence. "Hit!"

Bauer heard the German soldiers closing in. And then more German voices screaming, "Riflemen, this way! Quickly! Get the imposter!"

Bauer reached for his hip and writhed in pain on the ground. He watched as the remaining German soldiers abandoned the fence to chase after Beck. He saw Beck running past the village road into a wooded area on the other side yelling, "Catch me! Catch me!"

As Bauer began to lose consciousness, he heard shots fired and watched as Beck dropped to the forest floor.

"I got him! I got him!"

Bauer saw the soldier in the distance standing over Beck's prone body. He watched the soldier plunge his bayonet into Beck once and then once again. "Got him! I got him!"

Levinsky crawled on his stomach through the fence, pulled through by Clef.

"Hurry! We must go, now! Hurry!"

Levinsky made it through the fence and began to crawl toward the other men at the edge of the woods. He looked back, instinctively, and saw Bauer writhing in pain on the ground.

Clef whispered loudly, "Forget the soldier! Hurry! Hurry!"

Levinsky turned, followed Clef, and began crawling toward freedom. And then he stopped. "No. No. We go back. He's with us."

Clef grumbled loudly. "What? No. No. He's just a German soldier!"

"We must! He's one of us! We must!"

Clef sighed, angrily. "Then make it fast or we all die! Very fast!"

As Clef held back the fence, Levinsky crawled back through the opening and grabbed Bauer by his arms, pulling at his arms, struggling, and pulling some more. Bauer tried desperately to help by pushing himself forward.

They heard more German voices, growing in volume. "You, stop those men at the fence!" Gunshots and the sounds of frenzied German shepherds pierced the twilight sky.

By an act of will, Levinsky and Clef pulled Bauer through the fence, stood him up, one on each side, and stumbled their way to the woods under the sounds of gunfire.

...

The men followed Clef and the waiting driver through the woods to the nearby truck. Levinsky and Wenig held Bauer on each side, making their way as quickly as possible.

"Bauer, did Beck make it?"

"No, Levinsky. Beck is dead. I saw him shot. Then bayoneted twice. He's gone."

"Shit!" Levinsky was thinking that he wouldn't know what to do now without Beck. He had never considered it. He had always presumed that Beck would be there with them. He felt a sudden despairing loss. An encompassing sadness. His eyes welled with tears.

Bauer panted and said, "Let's stop just for a moment. I need to catch my breath."

As the three paused, Levinsky thought he saw something out of the corner of his eye. Something blazing and bright. And so white and beautiful. He looked more closely and saw a small bird, a white bird like a dove. It was resting on a tree branch. It began to sing sweetly. Levinsky stared in wonder. Seeing the white bird gave him an overwhelming sense of hope. Of happiness even. Of peace. He took a deep breath. He smiled to himself. Instinctively he waved a hello to the bird. He wasn't sure why. The bird seemed to understand, nodded, and flew away, gently singing.

"Levinsky, I said I think we can go now."

"Oh. Yes, Bauer. Yes." They caught up with the others who were now back at the truck, exhausted but free.

...

In the facility's waiting room, Rachel looked at her phone again. She was beginning to fear that something had happened, maybe a medical emergency. *No,* there would have been buzzing alarms and raised voices. Things were quite calm. But the kids had finished all their snacks and were beginning to throw their crayons at each other. *What's taking Nathan so long?*

"Kids, be nice. Daddy won't be long."

She looked back up to the lounge TV screen and its constant feed of CNN with text captioning. The same stories they had just shown. She didn't want to, but ...

"Okay, kids. Daddy has been a long time with Saba, so we're going to go back and see what's going on."

As she entered the room, she was shocked to find both Nathan and Saba holding hands and weeping gently. She had never seen Nathan cry.

Nathan looked up, tearfully, to see Rachel. "I'm so sorry, honey. I'm sorry. Saba had something important to tell me. It ... it's something wonderful and amazing. His story. I can tell you more when we are all home."

They continued to grasp hands and weep. "Saba, I promise you that this will be a part of our Passover stories. Something we'll remember forever."

Levinsky sighed. "Good, Nathan, good. About the white bird." He had said the words in German, "weißer vogel."

Rachel said, "Oh. Now I get it. 'Weißer vogel.' Clarissa thought Saba was saying, 'wife of Fogle.'"

Nathan nodded. "Yes, that's what Saba was trying to say." He looked over to his family, gratefully.

"Saba, we will forever remember your story. A story of bravery. A story of freedom. Our freedom to cherish, forever."

Levinsky nodded, "Yes, Nathan. And of peace. A story of peace."

ABOUT THE AUTHOR:

J. Paul (J.P.) Rieger is a mostly retired Maryland attorney and author of four novels, *The Case Files of Roderick Misely, Consultant,* a mystery featuring a wannabe lawyer first published in April, 2013; *Clonk!,* a police farce set in Baltimore and published in May, 2023 by Apprentice House Press (Loyola University, Maryland); *The Big Comb Over*, a slipstream comedy of manners published in May, 2024; and *Sunscreen Shower*, a *Clonk!* sequel, published in October, 2024 by Flock Publishing. Paul and his spouse live in Towson, Maryland. His website is jpaulrieger.net